THE FRAGMENT

THE
FRAGMENT

DAVIS BUNN

Franciscan
MEDIA
Cincinnati, Ohio

Cover design and illustration by Candle Light Studios
Book design by Mark Sullivan

Library of Congress Control Number: 2015960017

ISBN 978-1-63253-084-4 (hardcover edition)
ISBN 978-1-61636-934-7 (paperback edition)

Published by Franciscan Media
28 W. Liberty St.
Cincinnati, OH 45202
www.FranciscanMedia.org

Printed in the United States of America.
Printed on acid-free paper.
16 17 18 19 20 5 4 3 2 1

: CHAPTER 1 :

:

When Muriel Ross turned twenty-three in the spring of 1923, it seemed as though the world spun frantically without her. The war was over, and the influenza epidemic had eased. Great events were taking place everywhere except in her own small world. She was a child of the century, and she feared she was destined to remain an observer on the sidelines of life.

Her hometown of Alexandria seemed trapped in the amber of complacency. Her mother's greatest concern was that Muriel seemed to show no interest in men. It was, of course, utterly untrue that Muriel was not interested in them. She just simply did not want to wed a smug and contented Virginia gentleman, who would anchor her even more firmly into a world that stubbornly refused to turn.

And then in the space of three short months, everything changed.

The transformation came so rapidly that every morning upon awakening she had to remind herself that she was free. Free to explore the world. Free to spread her wings and soar further and higher than she had ever imagined possible. Free to experience the events she had once only read about in the newspapers and journals. Free to walk down the stairs and have breakfast in a Paris café. Which was precisely what she did.

Her small hotel was around the corner from the U.S. ambassador's residence. Her host, Senator Thomas Bryan, was the ambassador's guest. Muriel had only been in Paris for three days, and already she had her favorite table. She sat one row back from the street, in the right corner where the sun first emerged after cresting the rooftops. The air was brisk for April, but on Senator Bryan's instructions, she had packed her heaviest coat, as well as scarves and mittens, items she only wore during the rare January freezes back home. Now she snuggled into the coat's bulky warmth and exchanged greetings with the gray-haired waiter.

"Will mademoiselle be having her customary breakfast of hot chocolate and croissant?"

"Yes, please."

"Perhaps she will consider having something more sustaining? We have fresh eggs from the country this morning."

"Just the croissant, please."

"As mademoiselle wishes." Despite his limp and his age, the waiter managed to turn his bow into a flirtatious act.

Muriel would never have imagined being so thankful for her college French teacher. The professor had insisted upon his students learning proper pronunciation as well as the grammar and had mercilessly eradicated his students' southern drawls. Though French had required twice the study of anything else, Muriel had endured four years of the professor, dreaming of this day—and fearing that it would never come—when she would sit and watch the Parisian world on parade.

By the time she finished her meal, the steamy chocolate that had been whipped to a liquid froth and the feather-light croissant that had been so saturated with butter her fingers glistened,

Muriel was eager to be on her way. She paid and thanked the waiter and chose her direction at random. Almost everywhere she walked was fascinating. The streets were filled with the aura of a different way of life.

Muriel took the small camera from her purse and fit the leather strap around her wrist. The Leica was the first ever designed to take high-quality pictures and still fit into the photographer's hand. Muriel put the light meter in her pocket. The camera and the meter had been her father's parting gifts for his photography-loving daughter. Muriel had spent hours and hours on the steamship voyage across the Atlantic learning to calculate the proper aperture and shutter speed when photographing with this new style of camera. Now it was almost second nature. This was essential for how she intended to spend her day. She needed to check the light, set the camera, and shoot before the people realized what was happening. Muriel was not after formal portraits. She wanted her pictures to reflect the life and people of Paris in as natural a setting as possible.

"Good morning, Miss Muriel! What a positive delight it is to see you out and about!"

The senator's booming voice halted foot traffic all around her. Muriel sighed her disappointment at not being able to walk alone. "Good morning, Senator."

"Where are you off to this fine morning?"

She held up her camera. "I wanted to try to capture some of the people in this early light."

"Might an old gentleman accompany you?"

She knew it was not right to lie, but she also knew she had no choice in the matter. "It would be my honor, Senator."

"You are so kind." He fell into step beside her. "Is that a new coat?"

"No, it's the same one I brought from Alexandria." But she had made some changes and was surprised that a man like Senator Bryan would notice.

"And that silk scarf, how lovely. Now I know for a fact I've not seen that before."

"I bought it from the street market yesterday." She touched the silk knotted about her throat. "It's second-hand, of course."

"And you paid next to nothing for it, I'm sure."

"Pennies," she confirmed.

"It suits you." He fell into step beside her. "Where are we going?"

"I have no idea."

"That is my kind of walk. Go with nowhere particular in mind and see what life presents us." He glanced at her. "I am certain there is something different about your coat."

"I copied the fashion I've been seeing in the people here," she confessed. "They can't afford new clothes, but they make the best of what they have. They take an old coat and tailor it to the latest style."

"You show remarkable awareness for having only been here three days, my dear."

Thomas Bryan was an elegant man with a patrician's air. No one would mistake him for anything other than what he was, a mover and a shaker from a long line of power brokers. Until elected as the junior senator from Virginia, he had run the law firm established by his great-grandfather. He served as a deacon in their Alexandria church and had had a life-long friendship with her father.

But she was not going to allow the senator's presence to

interrupt her. The light was too fine. And to his credit, Thomas Bryan did his best to vanish in plain sight. Once she started shooting, he slipped back a few steps and blended in with the surroundings.

Muriel had never seen anything like the Paris light. The air was alive with a wealth of colors, all of them as muted and fresh as an Impressionist painting. The sky was an artist's blue. She photographed a street sweeper, a bent old man with a youth's face and stonemason's hands, plying the broom in a sideways motion, like he handled a scythe. Sunlight caught the water pouring from a nearby hydrant, forming a reflection of the young-old man in the cobblestones.

As they walked away, Thomas Bryan said, "A penny for your thoughts."

She was too caught up in the images she had captured to be anything less than honest. "I was wondering about that man and how he came to be there."

"Do you often feel captivated by your subjects?"

"Only when the picture is real. No, that's not the correct word. When the picture…"

"When the photograph captures the one taking the picture," he said softly.

"Yes, that's it exactly. The street sweeper was so intent on his work he did not even see me. I took four pictures. How could someone be so focused on such a mindless task? I was standing right in front of him. He did not look over once."

"I doubt he even saw the street, much less you." The words turned Senator Bryan very grave. "My dear, have you ever heard of trench warfare?"

"Of course. It was in the papers almost daily."

"The Great War brought us many horrors. I lost a nephew to the trenches. He came home, but in body only. That young man sweeping streets back there reminds me of him."

"That sweeper was an old man!"

"My dear, I doubt very much he has seen his twenty-fifth birthday." Senator Bryan showed the somber expression of one accustomed to bearing the world's burdens. "France has a new prime minister by the name of Raymond Poincaré. Upon being appointed, his first decree was to hire veterans of the trenches for all such mundane jobs. He said that after they had sacrificed so much, the least France could do in return was offer them a semblance of human dignity."

Muriel thought of the image she had captured, as though the only way she could envision the sweeper was through the safety of her viewfinder. "That is so terribly sad."

"I could not agree more. And yet Poincaré has elevated himself in the eyes of many people, including myself, by recognizing this problem at all. Most of the world wants to pretend that the war is simply over, that the scars are healed, and that life goes on. The Parisians have a new name for this post-war era. They call it *les Années Folles*. The crazy, insane years. They are doing their best to pretend that there are no problems, no wounds, no pains."

Muriel halted and turned to face this man she hardly knew. She heard the rich timbre of a voice accustomed to addressing great crowds. Senator Thomas Bryan was in his late sixties, and the winds of time had left him slightly bowed. He carried a cane, though he seldom seemed to need it. And yet there was a fire in him, one normally hidden behind his genteel demeanor. But it was visible now, as powerful as rage. She found herself shivering in the cool morning air, as though touched by a storm that defied the lovely spring dawn.

"I cannot fault these people," the senator went on. "They have come terrifyingly close to utter ruin. Their nation was almost lost to the Weimar war machine. They are a proud race, and they have been humiliated and starved and beaten. Of course the French want to pretend that all is well. But simply wishing for a thing does not make it so. There are a number of young artists and writers who are gathering here in Paris. Some very talented Americans are among them, F. Scott Fitzgerald and Ernest Hemingway, to name just two. They call themselves and others finding their way after the war the Lost Generation."

Muriel asked quietly, "Why are you here?"

He refocused upon the day. "Eh, what's that?"

"With me. Here in Paris. Why are you spending time with me?"

His gaze tightened with approval. "Don't you think it's a little late to be asking this question?"

"I don't mean any disrespect," Muriel replied. "But none of this makes sense."

"Your parents didn't object to my reasoning. And neither did you, if I recall correctly."

She was frightened of biting the hand that had set her free. But she needed to know. And she detected a glint of admiration in his smoky gray gaze. She found the courage to continue in her honest vein. "I would have done anything to escape from Alexandria."

"Some would consider it a fine enough place to live. Many, in fact."

"For me it was a prison."

"Back to your question, Miss Muriel. Tell me why you *think* you are here."

It was something she had spent the entire voyage considering. "You told my parents that you intended to seek antiques. You required a photographer who had experience in art history. You needed someone who could not just record your purchases, but ensure they are indeed as the sales people claim."

"Europe is awash in artwork and treasures," he confirmed. "Most of the royal families of Eastern Europe have been dispossessed. The Romanovs of Russia have vanished. There has never been a better time for such acquisitions. I represent several museums, including your employer, the Smithsonian. All of this I told your parents. All of this is true."

"And if that is all there is to this journey, I am grateful for the chance to serve you. But…"

"Go on."

"I read the papers. I know there are momentous events unfolding. The details of the League of Nations are being discussed. The treaties regarding Germany's war repayments are being negotiated in London. The world is changing. And you are here. Walking the streets of Paris. With me. A nobody."

"Hardly no one, my dear lady."

"As near as," she persisted.

"Well, well. The chrysalis has begun to open."

"Excuse me?"

He was smiling openly now. "Never mind, my dear. The answer to your question is, how involved do you want to become?"

"I don't understand, Senator. I am already as involved as I can be."

"That is hardly the case, I assure you."

She felt the import of his question and shivered with anticipation. "I want to be as involved as I possibly can."

"Are you certain? Because I am not asking you a theoretical question. We are no longer safely hidden away in the Smithsonian library, young lady. This is not about information you might come across in some book."

"I understand. You want to know if I am ready to commit. And the answer is, that is what I want. More than anything."

"Even without knowing what is behind my question?"

"I have known you all my life. My father and mother trust you. As do I."

"Very well." He pulled the pocket watch from his vest, flicked open the gold case, snapped it shut, then gripped her elbow and steered her around. "In that case, we must change course. There is not a moment to lose."

"Where are we going?"

"To the center of Paris fashion. The Rue Cambon." He lifted his cane to hail a passing horse-drawn taxi. "We have precisely three hours to transform you into an American princess."

CHAPTER 2

S enator Bryan ordered the driver to take them to the first
arrondissement. Muriel had not ridden in a horse-drawn
carriage for years. Here in Paris, they were everywhere. Petrol,
the senator explained, was still hard to come by. The Germans
had destroyed most of the French refineries in their savage
retreat across the Verdun. The only three that remained were
in Marseille, and the rail lines connecting the capital to the
southern port were still damaged. The senator spoke in a light
tone of voice, but Muriel had the distinct impression the words
were a test. As though he was still trying to decide whether to
trust her, and with how much.

She saw that day very clearly, as though already she was
aware of the momentous changes ahead. She saw how the light
played against the stone buildings and how there was not just
one kind of Parisian who passed their carriage, but a multitude
of different peoples, all brought together by this strange and
wonderful city. She saw the cares they bore, the burdens and the
worries. She felt them in her heart, as though they shouted to
her as she passed.

She saw the careful manner in which the senator pretended
not to observe her. He wore a hand-tailored suit and highly

polished shoes, and his cane's handle was ivory carved in the form of a Byzantine cross. She knew with an otherworldly sense that she was passing into some new realm, and she knew it was exactly what she wanted, what she had spent years yearning for.

Muriel's excitement left her almost able to stop time. She could number the horse's plodding steps and find rhythm in the creak of the carriage wheels. She could taste the city's flavor and name everything except the mystery that lay ahead. She never wanted to lose this sense of being so alive.

In the space of twenty minutes, they journeyed to a different world. The Rue Cambon was utterly untouched by war or hardship. The people were elegant, the shops divine. They halted in front of a new type of clothing store called a designer boutique. Muriel had read about them but never dreamed a friend of her father would open the carriage door and say, "We have arrived."

"I can't possibly go in there."

"If you intend upon joining me in my quest, you must."

"Senator, you know very well I can't afford a hat pin in that shop."

"From this point on, Miss Muriel, you are in my employ." He beckoned to where a shop lady held open the door. "Come."

Once inside, they were greeted by a slender woman whose dark hair was bobbed just below her ears. She was the most elegant woman Muriel had ever seen. Every turn of her hand, the tilt of her chin, the way she fingered her pearls as she studied Muriel, all spoke of intense refinement. Muriel realized, "You are Madame Coco Chanel."

"That is correct. And you speak French. That is good, for I have no time for the English language. What is your name?"

"M-Muriel Ross, Madame Chanel."

"And this gentleman, why is he here?"

"S-Senator Bryan is my employer."

"Ah. So that is what such men are called in America." She slipped a hand into an unseen pocket and drew out a pack of Turkish cigarettes. Muriel watched, fascinated as Coco Chanel extracted one, for she had never seen a woman smoke. Coco Chanel flicked open a gold embossed lighter, then paused when the senator offered his hand.

"Allow me."

Coco Chanel handed over the lighter and studied the senator with intense dark eyes as he lit her cigarette. She breathed out the smoke, "Not without finesse, this one. You should keep him."

Senator Bryan said, "Please tell Madame Chanel that you need three outfits. One for travel, one for day wear, and one for the reception this evening."

Muriel was midway through the translation when it hit her. "Where is this reception?"

"At the Élysée Palace."

The name caught Coco Chanel's attention. "You go to the palace? When?"

"In four hours."

"Then we must begin, yes?" She inspected Muriel's form with a clinical eye. "Tell me, Miss…"

"Muriel."

"Yes. Tell me, Muriel. What is it you do? Are you occupied with a professional life?"

"I serve as a historical researcher for the Smithsonian."

"This is what, exactly?"

"It is both a museum and a research institute, run by the government." Muriel tried to follow the designer tracking slowly around where she stood. "You could say it's a combination of your National Gallery and the Louvre."

"No, no, don't move. Stand straight. Shoulders back. Good. It is strange. I thought perhaps you had an artist's air about you."

"I love to photograph."

"Just as I suspected. Very well. Tell your gentleman friend that I have a new line that I am in the process of designing. It is called ready-to-wear. I will allow you to be one of the first to present this to the world."

"He's not…" Muriel gave a silent sigh and decided the woman would not hear her if she protested. She translated for Thomas Bryan.

"Excellent," the senator plucked out his pocket watch. "How long until you are ready?"

"Tell this gentleman not to pop his watch at me. I am well aware of the time. You may also inform that he is free to go about his affairs."

Muriel did so and then asked the senator, "Don't you want to know how much it costs?"

"No, and neither do you. Is that clear? You are not to worry about the expense."

Muriel suspected that Madame Chanel understood far more than she let on, for the designer smiled slightly as she began taking measurements.

She listened to the designer's rapid-fire French, then translated, "Madame Chanel says I am to meet you at the palace. She will arrange for transport." Muriel blushed in the process of continuing her translation of Chanel's words. "She says I need instructions in cosmetics, which she will arrange. And my hair..."

Senator Bryan saved her the need to translate that Chanel thought her hairstyle was better suited as a forest haven for baby birds. Or squirrels, perhaps. "Tell Madame Chanel that I appreciate all she does to make you ready to meet the prime minister."

Whatever else the senator was about to say was halted by Chanel touching Muriel's waist and demanding, "What is this I feel here?"

"A corset."

"And what does a lady of your age need with whalebone and shoestrings? You have no waist to hold in. You will take it off."

"But..." Muriel had not been seen in public without a corset since she turned fourteen.

"Do not give me your buts. You are not here to buy a frock. You are here to be dressed by Madame Chanel. And I say the days of corsets are over. Pffft. Finished. Now tell this man to depart so we can get to work."

Senator Bryan did not wait for a translation. He bowed a farewell to them both. "Until later, my dear."

: CHAPTER 3 :

:

The Élysée Palace, the official residence of the French president, was only five blocks from the Chanel boutique on Rue Cambon. But Coco Chanel insisted that Muriel take a carriage. A lady of substance, she declared, did not arrive for any rendezvous on foot.

The carriage entered a cobblestone forecourt through massive double gates. Muriel knew the style of structure, of course. She had studied them in books. Many city palaces from the pre-Napoleon eras copied the style of country estates called *manses*, from which came the English word *mansion*. The servants' quarters were in the building fronting the street, with the formal entrance carved from its center. The side buildings housed stables and chambers for the military guard. The carriage halted before two soldiers whose breastplates and helmets shone in the dusky light. One saluted as he opened her door, asked her name, and repeated it to a footman, who checked it in a leather-bound book.

She was passed to a second footman stationed just inside the main portal. He bowed as he ushered her inside, beckoning with white-gloved hands for her to follow him. She walked down a hall lit by ranks of crystal chandeliers to where a lean gentleman with the manner of an impatient general watched her with a cold eye. Muriel knew this man had to be the palace's majordomo. She had read of such men. She knew he would be a retired officer with a distinguished career, most likely from a noble family who had fallen on hard times. He would have become accustomed to being invisible to most of the people who paraded through these elegant chambers. From his frigid manner, Muriel sensed he accepted the repeated insult in silence but disliked it intensely. Muriel did the first thing that came to mind, which was to gather up the hem of her frock and curtsy.

"Mademoiselle is twenty-seven minutes early."

"Forgive me, sir. I completed my errands and had nowhere else to go."

"It is certainly better to be early than late," he allowed. He snapped his fingers at the hovering footman. "Show mademoiselle to the Sun Room and see to her needs."

"Monsieur is too kind." She accepted his cold nod with a smile, then turned away, thinking that her mother would be proud of how she had handled that one.

Muriel was ushered into a vast chamber whose tall windows with golden drapes captured the sunset and transformed it into a myriad of rose-tinted hues. The wall opposite the windows was dominated by a carved marble fireplace as large as a closet. To either side rose silver-backed mirrors, set strategically so that the afternoon light was magnified. The ceiling was adorned with gilded carvings that shone like veins of pure gold. Muriel refused the footman's offer of a drink and waited as he bowed and shut the double doors. Then she turned to greet the stranger in the mirror.

In Washington, the style of women's clothes was very much the same as it had been before the Great War. Layers of taffeta and crinoline formed broad skirts and clenched the body with starched fierceness. What Muriel wore now could not have been more different.

Her new dress was deceptively simple, with padded shoulders from which the dress descended in gentle waves around her body. The midnight blue Shantung silk captured the light in shimmering undulations. The fabric was caught at her ribcage and again upon her right hip. It formed suggestions of her femininity and yet remained utterly modest. Her hair had been cut and shaped by an impatient gentleman who had argued bitterly with Madame Chanel and refused to speak with Muriel at all. Her normally tight brown curls were opened up such that they tumbled in careful abandon about her shoulders. Her eyes were turned huge by the slightest hint of shadow and rouge. Her lips were…

Muriel had no choice but to turn away. The stranger in the mirror challenged her in a way she had never thought possible.

She walked to the western window. Her face was bathed by the setting sun. She felt captured by the light and the sudden wash of memories, all of them turned gold by the chamber where she stood. She recalled a certain day, just eleven weeks and a lifetime ago. She had been arguing with her mother over breakfast. Muriel had called it an argument then, and she still did now, though her mother would have described it as polite conversation. And on the surface that was all it had been, a mother enquiring and a daughter responding.

It had been the same conversation they had had many times before, only this had been the first time Muriel had actually recognized it as a trend. Her mother said she was just trying to understand. Why was her daughter leaving to take the train and go to work at the Smithsonian? Why did she hide herself away in the museum's dank cellar, with only books and scrolls and dusty artifacts for company? Why did she not want to lunch with the son of their close friends, who was a dentist and had met Muriel at a tea dance and found her most attractive? What was so fascinating about this research of hers that she would sacrifice the chance for a husband and a proper future? In truth, her mother had no interest in understanding at all. They both knew this. What her mother wanted was for Muriel to put aside her foolishness and settle down.

Muriel had endured the discussion as she had the ones that had marked so many other mornings. They had started when Muriel had insisted upon studying at Georgetown College. That was the same month when Tennessee had become the thirty-sixth state to ratify the Nineteenth Amendment, granting women the right to vote. Muriel had thought it was a day to celebrate, a day she would never forget. Her mother, whom Muriel loved very much, could not understand what all the fuss was about.

They had another such conversation when she worked a summer as a research fellow. The discussions had become even more insistent when Muriel had been introduced by Senator Bryan to the Smithsonian's chief archivist, who had offered her a job as a researcher. Every few months, her mother's impatience bubbled over, and she punctuated her daughter's morning with questions for which Muriel had no answer save one. She wanted more out of life.

That morning Muriel had left the house and taken the tram into the city. She had entered the Smithsonian's main building, descended the stone stairs, and entered the chamber that housed the research staff. The cavernous room was lined with shelves of tractates and bound documents and books. Muriel occupied an alcove similar to a medieval scribe's desk. Hers was the middle of a line of fourteen alcoves. The long table held all the researchers assigned to the era known as Late Antiquity.

Muriel's alcove had walls like wooden wings so that when she drew in close to the table she could not see anyone else. She faced five shelves crammed with documents and tomes. Her specific area of study was reliquaries. She had been assigned this task when she had been hired. She might well spend the next thirty years doing nothing else.

Muriel had wasted the entire morning mentally arguing with her mother and with herself. The room where she had sat that day was whitewashed stone. There were a series of small wire-mesh windows set high up in just one wall. They were meant to let in light, but that morning the windows only accented the fact that she was destined to spend the next three decades trapped twenty feet below ground level.

Muriel was abruptly brought back to the present by a soft knock upon the main doors. A white-gloved attendant opened the gilded portals, and Senator Bryan strode in. In the background, Muriel heard musical conversation. Senator Bryan stopped dead in his tracks, studied her a long moment, then smiled and declared, "My dear, you look positively alluring."

"I am dreaming," Muriel replied. "None of this is real."

"Take a long breath. Sip the air like vintage champagne," he said. "Enjoy this to the fullest. For it is more than real. It is only the beginning."

She felt a tremor take hold and rise through her. "Why am I here?"

He offered his arm. "Come and see."

: CHAPTER 4 :

:

The reception took place in an audience hall that could have held three of Muriel's entire home. Each arriving guest placed a calling card on a silver salver held by a footman. The major-domo accepted the card and announced them in a coldly sonorous voice. Muriel studied the people as the line snaked forward. Two of the receiving women were adorned with slender crowns. One of the gentlemen wore a general's uniform and bristling sideburns. Another bore the marshal's tricolor ribbon draped across his chest. Many women in the line ahead of Muriel had velvet gloves reaching almost to their elbows. A number of the guests inspected Muriel's gown, the men approving, the women coldly assessing.

As they approached the start of the receiving line, a footman raced down the hall and addressed the senator in rapid-fire French.

Muriel translated, "There is a messenger from the American embassy."

"What, here?"

"By the front portal. The footman says it is urgent."

"My dear, forgive me, but I must see what this is about."

"But what am I supposed..." Muriel watched him scurry

away. All her calm vanished. She was surrounded by people with whom she had nothing in common. She had never felt more out of place in her entire life.

The majordomo cleared his throat. "Perhaps mademoiselle would allow me the honor?"

For an instant, Muriel had no idea what he was talking about. Then he cocked his elbow in her direction. "Oh, thank you."

He motioned for the footman to set aside his salver and take over the announcements. "Forgive me, your name?"

"Muriel Ross. Of Alexandria. Might I ask yours?"

"Colonel Antoine, late of Lyon." The majordomo was an inch shorter than she was, but he emanated such authority he might as well have been ten feet tall. "How shall I present you?"

"I am a research fellow at the Smithsonian Institute in Washington."

"Most interesting work, I am sure."

"Not really." They took another step forward. It seemed to Muriel that every eye in the room was upon her now. "I spend my days inspecting and classifying articles almost two thousand years old."

"Sometimes, mademoiselle, the only way to understand the present is through the lens of the past." Another step. "A lesson too many of our leaders have forgotten."

"You fought in the Great War?"

"From the very first day." Another step. "To the final truce."

She struggled to find a proper response and settled upon, "I thank you for your sacrifice."

When he did not respond, Muriel feared she had said something wrong. But it was too late to apologize, for they arrived at the first hostess, a rather dumpy woman in a tiara. "The

Countess Maria of Fontainebleau. May I have the pleasure of presenting Professor Mademoiselle Ross of the United States, guest of Senator Bryan."

The woman cast a frosty eye over Muriel's dress and demanded, "Does the lady speak French?"

The majordomo responded for her, "Most suitably, your highness."

"Professor of what?"

Muriel started to protest that she held no such lofty position. But they were already moving on to the next person, the gentleman with the tricolor banner across his chest. Muriel was unable to correct the misunderstanding, as she scarcely had time to greet each person before being passed on to the next individual. Finally they arrived before the last man in the receiving line. He was slender to the point of emaciation, and his black suit was adorned with no decoration of any kind. Yet he radiated a sense of great force, tight and bleak and utterly focused. The majordomo bowed and said, "Prime Minister Poincaré. Your Excellency, may I introduce—"

"*Mademoiselle* Ross," Muriel insisted and dropped into the deepest curtsy of her entire life. "A mere research fellow. It is such an honor, Your Excellency."

"A most remarkable young lady, Excellency," the majordomo murmured.

"Is she indeed?" The premier's voice was no less imposing for his gentle tone. "Where are you a fellow and in what subject?"

"The Smithsonian, Excellency. In late antiquities."

"What epoch precisely?"

"Late Roman and early Byzantine. I study reliquaries."

"Do you indeed?" The reception line had come to a complete halt. The entire world seemed to have stopped. Everyone forced to wait while the newly appointed premier of France spoke with her. "How are you finding Paris, mademoiselle?"

She felt his gaze boring into her and knew this was what it meant to stand in the presence of power. "It is beyond my wildest dreams, Excellency."

"What in particular has captured your fancy?"

She searched frantically for something suitable. "The people. They...they have been through so much. They have endured the impossible. And now they laugh. They live. They find joy in a beautiful spring day." She took a shaky breath. "They are the bravest and most wonderful people in the entire world."

His gaze softened momentarily. "I could not agree more. I wish you a pleasant evening. And mademoiselle."

"Excellency?"

"Inform Senator Bryan that the request he made of me has met with my approval."

• • •

As Muriel was escorted across the marble floor, a footman rushed forward and whispered urgently to the majordomo. The gentleman bowed and excused himself and rushed away, leaving Muriel very alone. The party swirled around her and left her untouched. The senator did not return.

Muriel felt isolated by the laughter and the talk that did not include her. She sensed that it would be wrong to leave, and yet she wanted desperately to go. She felt like an imposter, like she wore someone else's clothes, like she stood in someone else's life.

"Forgive me, Mademoiselle. You are the senator's niece?"

She scarcely saw who spoke. "We are no relation, Monsieur."

"Of course. I just…" He cleared his throat. "Colonel Antoine asked me to say that the senator has been forced to return to your embassy. He will join you directly."

"Thank you, monsieur." Muriel sighed inwardly. She tried to tell herself that there were worse fates than being a wallflower in a French palace.

"Can I get you something, Mademoiselle?"

"No, thank you." She realized he was doing his best to be friendly. "I don't belong here."

"That makes two of us, Mademoiselle."

She studied him. His height and severe manner were accentuated by the formal dress. A pair of scars climbed from his collar. One sliced below his left ear and disappeared in his hairline. The other carved a niche from his jawline and stabbed a point in his right cheek. "You were in the war?"

"There is no *was*," he replied softly. "It is with me still."

Despite the tragic quality of his words, the raw truth was refreshing. "I cannot imagine what it must have been like."

"No," he agreed. "You cannot."

She offered her hand. "I am Muriel Ross."

His hand was cool and strong like a rapier, which he resembled. All tensile strength and deadly force. "A distinct honor, mademoiselle. Charles Fouchet, at your service."

She found herself drawn to his quiet strength. There was something decidedly French about the tight way he held himself inside, a passion and a force that were barely contained within the tailored evening clothes. His eyes sparked with a feverish intensity, and yet his manners were impeccable, his voice a melody. Muriel asked, "If you do not belong, why are you here?"

"I serve at my master's pleasure." He indicated the stout gentleman at the center of the receiving line. "Maurice Maunoury is minister of the interior. I am his private secretary."

"How does one come to hold such a position?"

"I was with his son at the academy." His words became clipped. "We were the closest of friends. His son did not come home. The war and the influenza...cost me everything. The minister has done what he can to grant me a future."

"I am sorry for your loss, Monsieur."

He bowed stiffly. "Mademoiselle is too kind."

"No, I mean it. Truly. It is terrible what you and your people have suffered. The war and then the influenza epidemic. I see the strains on so many faces. Including yours. France is a country made for song and joy. Paris is a city of lights. This darkness does not belong."

His gaze tightened further, as though he sought to peel away the layers and see to the heart of her. "Why are you here, mademoiselle?"

"I have no idea."

"I do not mean tonight. I mean here. In Paris."

"The answer is the same, Monsieur Fouchet. I was a researcher at the Smithsonian Institute in Washington. The senator convinced them to grant me leave. He represents my institute and several museums. He says he needs me to help him verify the quality of certain antiquities." She hesitated.

"But you suspect something else is behind your journey."

"There are many older and more qualified experts who would be thrilled to help him. Such an assignment could open many doors. I could be appointed to a research fellowship at a university. I could return to a senior position at some museum."

"What is your specialization?"

"Late Roman and early Byzantine antiquities. Currently, I study reliquaries. These are vessels designed to hold items from the church's earliest era. Some of these vessels are uniquely beautiful. And valuable."

"I know what a reliquary is."

"You are a student of antiquities?"

"Not exactly. You see, my role…"

Senator Bryan rushed over. "My dear Miss Muriel, I cannot tell you how sorry I am. An urgent matter arose that could not wait."

"I understand. Senator Bryan, may I introduce Charles Fouchet, private secretary to the interior minister."

Senator Bryan showed genuine astonishment. "But that is not possible!"

"Monsieur?"

"You are the very person I wanted Miss Muriel to meet!"

CHAPTER 5

The American Cathedral in Paris was the head of all the Episcopal churches in Europe. It was located on Avenue George V, one of the city's most fashionable boulevards. The simple façade was little more than a stone wall, a single narrow stained-glass window, and a portal. This entry opened into a stone courtyard, with the church itself on the right and the vicarage on the left. The church's interior was classically beautiful, a rare gem that did not seek to overwhelm. The service that Sunday morning was packed. Senator Bryan remained very preoccupied throughout. He rose and knelt and sat with the others, but did not sing, and from his vacant expression Muriel suspected he did not hear a word.

Afterward, the senator apologized that an urgent matter had arisen, and he had to meet with the ambassador. Muriel returned to her hotel and changed into clothes from home. The bags and boxes delivered from Chanel's boutique remained piled in one corner of her closet. When she pulled out the case holding her camera equipment, she paused a moment to caress the evening gown's shimmering fabric. The previous evening already felt like a dream from someone else's life.

She walked for hours and shot three rolls of film. Kodak had recently invented a new type of film, intended to bring professional quality pictures into the hands of amateurs like herself. Muriel was delighted to find a shop near the Quai d'Orsay that stocked it. The rolls were three times the cost of normal film, but she felt as though she was capturing dreams to last a lifetime and wanted the finest quality product to hold them.

When she returned to the hotel, she discovered the senator pacing on the sidewalk in front of the entrance. "Where on earth have you been?"

"Walking." She held up her camera. "Taking pictures."

"Never mind that. Come on, we don't have a moment to lose!"

"But...I must change clothes."

"No time for that!" He bundled her into a waiting hansom cab and ordered her to tell the driver to make all possible haste.

Muriel asked, "Where are we going?"

"The Abbey of Saint Denis. You have heard of it?"

"Of course. But what is the hurry?"

"Listen very carefully. We have an opportunity. No, scratch that. We *may* have an opportunity. It is why I made this journey. Your conversation with the prime minister has opened a door. Perhaps."

"I-I don't understand."

"Everything I told you and your parents is true. We are here in search of antiquities. *One* item, to be precise. One very precious, rare item."

The idea came to her in a flash of sunlight, in the hasty drumbeat of the horse's hooves. "A reliquary."

"Precisely."

"Did you arrange for my research assignment at the Smithsonian?"

"I merely made a suggestion to the director. In case this item did indeed surface."

"How long have you been hunting for this reliquary?"

"All my adult life." He was a man transformed. Gone was the polished and urbane man of power. In his place sat a man on fire with a passion that defied his years. "I heard of this when I was in university. Something spoke to me. I would like to think it was God. But all I can say for certain is that I knew at that very moment this quest was to play a vital role in my life."

She felt the electric pulse of his zeal deep inside and shivered. "What does the reliquary contain?"

Before he turned to her, before he spoke, she knew. There was only one article that could so transform this man, lift him from the realms of earthly power, and catapult him into a hunt that had occupied him for decades.

"The True Cross," he replied. "Perhaps. And if so, we are on the trail of a fragment that has been lost for over a thousand years."

: CHAPTER 6 :

:

Muriel had studied the Abbey of Saint Denis for years. She had sifted through all the many legends and distilled elements of truth about the church's very distant beginnings. The stone arch fronting the street was flanked by officers in the sweeping capes of the government's security brigade. Senator Bryan showed them a document, and then he and Muriel were saluted inside. The path wound through a tiny patch of garden fronting several magnificent buildings. They approached the cloister just as the sunset laid a golden hand upon the western roofs. Muriel entered the nave and gasped.

The church stood upon the earliest known Christian cemetery in France. The original edifice was constructed in the year 475, then replaced in 690, and then rebuilt in its current form in 1135. The structure began the style known as Gothic architecture. The church had been a pilgrimage site for over fifteen hundred years and was the burial place of nearly every French king from 930 to 1800. But none of this was what took Muriel's breath away.

After entering the nave, Muriel moved forward only because Senator Bryan pulled on her hand and directed her into a pew. But all she saw was light transformed by stained glass.

The church was quite large and could easily have held several hundred penitents. Yet it seemed strangely intimate, almost as though it had been designed just for her, a place where she could sit in wonder and awe.

The stone walls formed intricately carved frames for the stained glass. The entire nave was rimmed by glass, tall narrow windows that rose from waist height to the distant ceiling. The sunset washed through the western casements and bathed them in all the tones of the rainbow. A choir stood at the front of the church, their white cassocks transformed into hues of purple and rose. They sang a Brahms chorale.

Muriel felt as though the light and the chamber granted her an ability to truly join with the others gathered here. She studied the faces and saw the years of strain and hunger and tension ease away, replaced by a peace so intense it created a sense of humble reverence within herself.

As with all young Americans, the Great War had shaped her teenage years. But the events had remained at a vast and safe distance. Here the trauma was fully revealed. And yet somehow these people had managed to hold on to faith and hope, despite everything the conflict had hurled at them. She saw men and women alike wipe away tears and wished she dared to pull the camera from her pocket and take their pictures. But she could not disturb their moment. For it truly was theirs. She was merely a visitor, here for a brief instant, allowed to glimpse their rebirth of hope.

When the concert ended, Senator Bryan leaned toward her and murmured, "Whatever it was you said to the premier, however you influenced him, I need you to do this again now."

Before she could ask what that meant, he rose and beckoned her forward. Because they had arrived late, they had been seated with the members of the public. The people's dress and mannerisms changed as she stepped forward. The crowd became more polished, more refined. Muriel found herself very glad they had not been seated among these people.

Standing at the dais was the choir director and two priests. One was in full regalia, his white cassock overlaid by a long silk stole sewn with what appeared to be solid gold thread. A heavy jeweled tassel dangled from each end. The man was portly and somewhat flushed and gave a high nasal twist to his words.

Standing to his right was a second priest, this one wearing an austere black cassock. From his lapel dangled a small medal. Muriel had seen these before, worn by men and women alike in civilian garb. She knew they represented some high military honor and were worn with great pride. The man had a long beaked nose and craggy features. His gray eyes were almost hidden beneath scraggly eyebrows. They held a gentle light, but Muriel supposed the man could turn frightful and fierce when provoked.

Standing just behind them, almost as though he sought to vanish in the shadows, was Charles Fouchet, the intense young man she had met at the reception. She wondered whether she should greet him, but just then Senator Bryan said, "My dear, I would like to introduce you to a great friend of America, Bishop Suget, prior of the Notre Dame Cathedral."

To her surprise, he indicated not the priest in fine regalia, but the man standing next to him. "An honor, Monsieur Bishop."

"Ah, you speak French."

"Poorly, Monsieur Bishop. For which I apologize."

"Far better than my English, I assure you. This is my friend, Father Ricard, prior of Saint Denis."

"Thank you for the most delightful performance, in the most exquisite surroundings."

"Mademoiselle." He frowned at her muddy coat and stained shoes. Only the priest's eyes and mouth were small. The rest of him was so well padded his chin formed a tiny bump at the bottom of his face.

Bishop Suget indicated the man standing behind him. "The young gentleman has passed on a request from the interior minister."

"Most irregular," the prior stormed. "Out of the question."

"And yet the prime minister himself seems to feel we should grant this appeal. Is that not so, Monsieur Fouchet?"

"Indeed, Bishop Suget."

"A personal request from the interior minister, with whom I served in the army, backed by the prime minister certainly deserves our attention, would you not agree, Father?"

The priest had very cold eyes. Muriel might have been worried by his evident animosity, except he chose that moment to frown. His little mouth puckered into a bow, small as an infant's.

"You are Catholic, Mademoiselle?"

"Methodist, Sir."

The priest snorted. "Scandal."

But the bishop seemed to find the priest's displeasure humorous. "This is your first trip to Paris?"

"My first trip anywhere, Sir.

He crossed his arms. "Tell me the one thing that has impressed you the most since your arrival."

"Paris has many populations, or so it seems to me. But one heart. I find myself drawn to Paris and its people in a way that I have never felt before."

He studied her. "This religion of yours, it is not merely a title? By this I mean, you are truly a believer?"

"My faith in Jesus is very important to me, sir."

The priest muttered, "A Protestant believer."

This time she was certain a smile flickered across the bishop's features. There and gone in an instant. "Might I ask, have you perhaps also learned something from the French and their faith?"

This time she did not need to think. "To hope in the face of hardship. To believe when all the world is wrapped in darkness. To search..."

"Yes, go on, I'm waiting."

"To search for a light at the end of the darkness. And when it arrives, to allow yourself to smile again. And laugh. And sing. And defy the sorrows and the memories, and sit in a beautiful church, and watch the light transform the passing day, and lose yourself in the joy of Brahms."

The bishop studied her for a long moment, then said, "Notre Dame, my office, eight-thirty tomorrow morning. Good day, Father. Thank you for a lovely concert."

This time the priest waited until the bishop had left the nave to declare, "Scandal!"

• • •

But the day was not over yet. As they emerged from the church compound, Charles Fouchet moved up alongside her and said, "You handled yourself most suitably with the bishop, Mademoiselle."

"Monsieur is too kind." Muriel allowed herself to be steered through the portal and down a few steps along the tree-lined avenue. "Excuse me for not greeting you earlier, sir. I felt... constrained."

"I understand." For all his dark intensity, Charles Fouchet had a surprising smile. It stretched his face in unaccustomed angles. Muriel had the impression he revealed the man he had once been. Back before the world went insane. "I am invited to a tea dance and was wondering if I might..." He broke off at the senator's approach.

"Forgive me, my dear. But we must be off."

"Monsieur Fouchet has invited me to tea."

"Out of the question. Forgive me, sir. But the lady's time is limited, today of all days."

Charles Fouchet hid his disappointment beneath a bow. "I understand."

"Perhaps another time. Come, my dear. We must be off."

She found herself sharing Fouchet's disappointment. "I am so sorry, Monsieur."

He saw something in her face that caused him to smile once more. "At least I shall have the pleasure of your company tomorrow. The minister will want me to observe."

"I shall look forward to it very much."

He bowed again, this time to kiss her hand. "I bid you adieu."

Senator Bryan led her to the waiting transom and demanded, "Must you charm every gentleman whose path you cross?"

"You obviously are mistaking me for someone else."

He huffed softly, thumped his cane upon the carriage floor, and asked, "What is the finest camera in the world?"

Muriel did not need to ponder that. "A Graflex Speed Graphic. It has a hand-ground lens and uses three-and-a-quarter- by four-and-a-quarter-inch plates."

"Ask the driver where we can find one."

She gaped at him. "Sir, you cannot be serious. The apparatus costs more than a new car."

"Never mind that. We must have one, and today."

"On a Sunday?"

"If it is as expensive as you say, the shop owner will only be too happy to assist us."

She discussed it with the driver, who nodded and cracked his whip. Muriel leaned back in her seat and stared out the side window. But for once, she was unable to concentrate upon the city or the people.

The swirl of events coalesced into a sudden revelation, one that blinded her to the outside world. The senator's time and attention, the clothes, the reception, the people, and now this. Traipsing about Paris searching for the finest camera in the world. Some other woman might have been thinking that her time had arrived. She was being handed her lifelong dreams on a silver platter. And perhaps later she might even dare thinking this herself. But just then she was consumed by one terrifying thought after another.

The senator and all these other people were paying her attention because they thought she was someone other than who she was. They considered her some kind of expert. They deemed her sophisticated. They saw a woman of letters, able to manage herself on the world's stage. But Muriel knew it was not merely the fancy Chanel gown that created a false impression. She had been thrust into a situation which she did not understand, and most certainly did not feel ready to face.

Over and over her mind echoed to one single refrain, drummed into her by the horse's hooves and the wheels clattering over the rough streets.

What would happen if she failed?

: CHAPTER 7 :
:

When Muriel came downstairs the next morning, Charles Fouchet was seated in the hotel's cramped lobby, studying papers. When he saw her, he stuffed the papers back in the file and rose to his feet. "Good morning, Mademoiselle. Senator Bryan asks me to say he has been unavoidably detained. He will meet us at the cathedral. He asked the minister if I might serve as your escort this morning."

"I apologize for troubling you, Monsieur."

"It is my sincerest pleasure. Might I please ask you to call me by my given name?"

"Very well, Charles. And I am Muriel."

"An excellent beginning to what might become an exceptional day." He reached out. "Shall I assist you with your equipment?"

"Thank you." She refused to release her new Graflex camera but gladly handed over the tripod and the leather case holding the light meter and the negative plates.

Charles frowned. "What has happened to your hands?"

"The new tripod pinched me before I got the hang of it."

"May I see?" He had a remarkably gentle touch. He inspected the point on her palm where the tripod had bitten deep. Then he noticed the blister on her forefinger and gave her a knowing look. "You practiced shooting photographs?"

"Most of the night," she confessed. "I wanted to become accustomed to this new equipment. It is much more complex than I imagined."

"I have seen similar injuries before. On the trigger fingers of soldiers growing accustomed to new weapons." He seemed reluctant to release her hand. "They were the ones most likely to survive."

She liked that so much she was able to confess, "I'm so frightened."

"What of?"

"I have no idea." She pointed at the front door. "Whatever waits for me out there."

He showed the rare ability to sympathize without condescending. "I would ask a favor, Miss Muriel. For this day, allow me to play the role of your humble servant. Whatever you require in the task ahead, turn to me, and I will see it is done. Anything. Even to simply offering you my confidence. For I know you will do well. I *know* this."

"Thank you," She whispered. "I accept."

He hesitated one instant, then added, "The senator asked me to convey one further message."

"You had best tell me, then."

"He expressed a keen desire that you wear one of the new frocks."

"No," she said. But the simple denial was not enough, given his offer of kindness. "It makes me feel like a fraud. I am not that woman."

"What woman is that?"

"A sophisticated lady of the Rue Cambon. I am Muriel Ross, late of Alexandria."

He revealed another of his rare smiles. "I shall have to apologize to the senator for having forgotten to mention his request."

The ministerial car stood almost as high as a carriage and was far more comfortable than the hansom cabs. The driver sat in a separate cabin exposed to the elements, while they were seated in leather-bound comfort encased by glass. Muriel wished she could set aside her anxieties and enjoy the view. But she knew that was impossible. Perhaps conversation would help quell her fears, at least for a moment. So she asked, "Do you know what has delayed Senator Bryan?"

"I do."

"Can you tell me what it is?"

"There are two matters. The senator represents your government in urgent negotiations over war reparations. You know what this is?"

She had followed the story with her father. "The debt Germany owes the nations upon whom it declared war."

"Germany's new postwar government has refused to pay. France needs the money desperately to rebuild the areas to the north that were destroyed by the trench warfare. Prime Minister Poincaré has decided to send troops into Germany to occupy the region across the border near Strasbourg until the funds have been repaid."

"But that is terrible!"

"Your government certainly thinks so. But as I said, Germany refuses to pay, and we must have the funds. We must."

She saw there was nothing to be gained from further protests. Charles's features had become stony, as though to repel any assault. She changed the subject, "And the second matter?"

"It has become increasingly evident that the Ottoman Empire is crumbling."

She had studied this issue as well. The empire was ruled from what once had been the world's first Christian capital city. She said, "The Ottoman Empire has stood on the brink of destruction longer than I have been alive. And the nations have worried over the fate of the Dardanelles for a century."

He examined her. "You are a most remarkable young lady. I doubt there are a handful of people in France who could find the Dardanelles on a map."

"I have been fascinated by the news since I was a child. What makes things different this time?"

"This time there is a young general by the name of Atatürk. He has managed to unite the various rebel factions and is marching upon Constantinople."

She was about to ask him what he was not saying, when he pointed ahead and said, "We have arrived."

• • •

The bishop's entrance to the Cathedral of Notre Dame was on the riverside, down a tight cul-de-sac tucked behind the nave. Muriel smelled the fragrance of springtime blossoms as she was ushered through a narrow iron gate and entered a small secret garden. From beyond the walls, she heard the barges chug along the languid Seine River. A bird hidden among the roses that climbed the side wall sang her a welcome.

She entered through a peaked door and walked a hallway adorned with religious paintings and a statue so old the kneeling woman's face had been washed away. Muriel then entered a parlor to find Father Ricard standing beside the unlit fireplace, his face ruddy with the ire that he silently directed at her. But

Senator Bryan remained unscathed by the priest's irritation, and Bishop Suget seemed even more amused than the previous day.

The bishop walked over and enveloped her hands in both of his, then introduced the three other men in the room: the abbot and the prior and the priest assigned to the cathedral. Muriel was the only woman present. It happened often enough. She was one of only three female researchers on the Smithsonian's staff. But today it only added to her nervousness. Charles Fouchet must have noticed, for he stepped in close behind her, close enough that she could smell his cologne, a fragrance of lemon oil and something vaguely exotic. She found herself steadied by his presence.

The bishop wasted no time. He led her through a rear entry and into a room lined by hooks holding the priests' regalia. As they passed down a second bare hallway, the bishop said, "There are those among us who feel I am making a serious mistake."

"This is a *French* moment," the priest of Saint Denis declared hotly. "A *Catholic* moment."

"But I, on the other hand, do not agree. I have prayed upon this much of the night. And I feel that it is a moment for all who appreciate freedom and have sacrificed to maintain it, a moment when all these should unite in joy and a hope for tomorrow." He paused with his hand upon the door at the hallway's end and smiled down at her. From the other side, Muriel heard the quiet sound of people's hushed voices. Many people. The bishop went on, "I feel this is a moment when all believers throughout the world, regardless of their denomination, should unite together beneath the banner of our one Lord."

He pushed open the door and ushered her through with a smile. "And my voice, I am happy to say, carries the determining vote."

The Cathedral of Notre Dame was filled to overflowing. The crowd stretched back to the open rear doors. They crammed the aisles and the courtyard beyond the portals.

"This way, mademoiselle."

The bishop led her across the nave and through the smallest door of all, set into the side alcove by the empty choir stall. He started down a narrow circular stairway. "Watch your step."

Notre Dame was so old its beginnings had been lost in the vague mists of legend. The earliest known church had been dedicated to the apostles and had been completed before the year 300. Five centuries later, Emperor Charlemagne stopped here to give thanks for his victory in unifying France. Muriel knew that recent excavations had found stones from the Merovingian Cathedral completed in the late 500s.

The Notre Dame Cathedral had been started in 1163 and completed by 1250, though extra features were added over the next hundred years. As she descended into the vaulted crypts, Muriel felt as though the present day had been peeled away, revealing the epochs that had come before. She passed the former burial chambers of knights and nobles. These vaulted chambers were now so filled with treasure and artifacts that the doors could not be sealed shut, and the wealth of centuries spilled into the main gallery.

Finally, they arrived at a massive door held open by a wrought iron chain. "This is the royal treasure room, home to some of France's most valued artifacts," the bishop said.

Muriel entered and heaved a sigh of relief, for the cellar's flickering lamps had been replaced by three lights on tall metal stands. The bishop smiled at her response and said, "I could not have my fellows laboring away in the dark, preparing for the moment when our treasure reemerges. They needed to see what they were doing." The bishop turned and asked a priest, "How much time do we have?"

"Forty minutes, Monsieur Bishop."

Suget told her, "I must ask you to hurry, Mademoiselle. In less than an hour, the service begins to commemorate the reliquary returning to public view for the first time in six years."

"Of course."

At the center of the light was a table, and on it was a tall artifact of some sort, hidden beneath a mantle of black velvet. She found her heart racing as the bishop walked over and pulled away the coverlet.

The reliquary of the True Cross stood almost three feet high. She had seen numerous drawings and even handled several replicas, one dating from the fourteenth century. Even so, the article took her breath away. It was fashioned from solid gold, the arms of the cross ending in the cloverleaf pattern of the Eastern church. At its heart was a clear crystal casing, as broad as her hand and standing eleven inches high. Inside was the piece of wood.

She of course knew its history. The majority of the cross found by Helena had been left at the Church of the Holy Sepulchre in Jerusalem. But one segment, perhaps a meter in length, had returned to Europe with her.

Once Helena's son had been named the first Christian emperor of the Roman Empire, Helena had sent fragments to each of the major church centers throughout the kingdom, marking the empire's coming transformation to a Christian nation, uniting them beneath the banner of the cross. This particular reliquary had been fashioned in the late twelfth century.

The bishop slipped on a pair of cotton gloves. "The key."

The priest of Saint Denis whined, "I must protest. This is..."

The bishop turned and silenced him with a single look. He then accepted the key from the prior and fitted it into a tiny hole in the reliquary's side. He opened a side panel and withdrew what at first glance appeared to be a small silver box. "This is what you came for."

The senator appeared at her side. She wanted to step over, grant him room. But just then her limbs refused to function.

"I must ask you not to touch this."

Muriel made do with a simple nod. She had heard of these but until this moment assumed it was a legend seventeen hundred years in the making. Helena was said to have encased the pieces of wood in silver inscribed with words from the book of John. There they were for her to read, the Greek letters carved by hand: *I am the true vine.*

The wood was brownish red, almost like it had been petrified. Which was impossible, of course. The process of petrification took far longer than several centuries. She knew it was most likely a patina of blood that concealed the grain.

Muriel felt the emotions well up in her like great waves, crashing upon her heart, sending her to her knees. Even then she could not take her eyes off the small sliver of wood. She had lived with her faith her entire life. She was a child of the church. And yet it seemed to her as though she had never experienced her Savior's gift in such a way as now.

: CHAPTER 8 :

:

Muriel used every remaining minute to both photograph and inspect the artifact. She was mildly aware that people moved about her. She took her pictures and adjusted the lights and took more. Then someone stepped up and offered to assist her, and she asked for notepad and pencil and magnifying glass. She had no idea who it was who handed her the items, only that they appeared. She ordered the lights drawn closer to the table. She used the glass and inspected the letters carved into the side of the silver case. She photographed three plates through the magnifying glass, and then, in case the pictures were not clear, she sketched the letters carved into the side of the silver frame and made notes of their dimensions. She then did the same with the wood itself, noting the brownish-red hue, the small spot where the wood's grain was visible, how edges still held the markings where the knife had carved out this segment. She noted how the frame's corners were sealed around the wood. She occasionally felt herself growing overwhelmed by what she studied. She refused to allow tears to blur her vision. She could almost hear the minutes ticking away. She would give in to her emotions once the opportunity was gone.

Some small part of her sought reasons why this was happening. The simplest explanation was that another reliquary had been identified, and they needed an expert who could authenticate it. This made a great deal of sense. Over the centuries, a number of duplicates had been made, some of immense value. But very few of the copiers would have had an opportunity to study either the wood or the original frame at such proximity. All this passed through her mind in fleeting snatches, quick as her tightly compressed breaths. Then she refocused upon what she studied, and everything else became lost. Inconsequential. Dismissed for another, less august time.

And then it was over. Muriel watched as the bishop replaced the silver case into the reliquary and locked the hidden portal. The velvet cloak settled over the reliquary, and a young priest picked it up by the base. Muriel noticed that the young priest's face was wet with tears. She liked that someone else felt engulfed by the power of this moment.

As they left the chamber, Muriel stopped in the doorway and looked back. The empty table stood beneath the lamp's glare. The air above the scarred wooden surface trembled slightly.

She followed the priests back up the curved stone stairway and across the nave and into a side alcove. The reliquary was settled upon the altar as the priests donned their formal robes. The prior of Saint Denis looked over at her several times. Muriel could feel the heat of his glare, but she did not care. She continued to stare at the velvet covering. There was room for nothing else.

She jerked slightly at a touch on her shoulder. The bishop was in his vestments, white and crimson and gold. Muriel thought his stern visage fit the station and the moment. He asked solemnly, "Do you wish to witness the unveiling?"

"Please," she whispered.

The bishop turned to the younger priest, who still bore the emotional weight of what he had carried. "Escort our honored guests into the church and find her a seat."

Senator Bryan spoke to her, something about needing to return to the embassy on a matter that could not wait. Muriel nodded without even seeing him. She did not want to allow any part of the outside world to interfere.

She left her camera and tripod in the sacristy but carried the case holding the plates. They would not leave her side until they were delivered to a trustworthy developer. The priest led them down the central aisle to the third row, which was occupied by church officials. He leaned over and whispered. Muriel heard him mention the bishop's name. The officials slid over, granting them room. Muriel slipped into the pew and thanked them in a voice she did not recognize as her own.

She did not try to follow the ceremony. She sat and knelt and stood, taking her cue from the people to either side. She studied the people around her and saw embedded in the faces an exquisite hunger, a beautiful yearning. She felt humbled by their courage. They dared to hope. They clung to faith.

The moment came when the choir's voice rose in passionate cadence, and the velvet coverlet was drawn back. The bishop lifted the reliquary up to the church. The air vibrated softly about the entire nave, or so it seemed to Muriel.

• • •

When the service was over, they returned to the sacristy, and Muriel retrieved her equipment. She tried to thank the bishop, who seemed to approve of her fumbling words. He took her hand in both of his and held it with the gentleness of a man offering a benediction. He wished her a safe journey, both in her quest and through her life. Muriel left the church feeling hollowed and overwhelmed at the same time.

The Notre Dame Cathedral fronted a small plaza. Traffic trundled along the road to her left, and beyond the road was the broad promenade lining the Seine. The plaza was rimmed by stalls, all of them selling religious articles and books. Muriel approached a booth selling crucifixes. "I wish to buy a cross."

"These I have." The woman was dressed for a far colder day, with a woolen scarf knotted over her hair and a heavy sweater covering her bulky frame. She indicated her wares with an arthritic gesture. "Will the lady have silver, perhaps? Or gold?"

"Something simple." Speaking the words should not cause her eyes to burn. "Something in wood."

"These are from petrified olive wood. Hand carved."

She felt the smooth surface, the subtle grain. The cross was suspended from a delicate silver chain. "I would like two, please."

The woman named a price. Muriel handed over the money without protest. The woman offered profuse thanks and asked, "You wish them wrapped?"

"I want to wear one. The other is a gift that doesn't need wrapping."

She handed them over. "You were inside?"

"I was, yes."

"You saw it?"

Muriel lifted her camera case. "They let me take photographs."

The woman's face was seamed and ingrained with what appeared to be soot. "Was it real, what they showed the people?"

"I can only say that the moment was a gift."

She seemed satisfied with Muriel's words. "Go with God, Mademoiselle."

"And you, Madame." Muriel walked back over to where Charles Fouchet stood holding her tripod. The rugged gentleman looked as drawn and fatigued by the experience as she felt. She handed him the second cross and said, "To commemorate this day."

He accepted it and studied the simple carving. "I shall treasure it, and this memory."

"As shall I."

They turned and walked toward the line of waiting taxis. Fouchet gave the driver the name of her hotel. As they settled inside, he confessed, "The invitation to a new life, a new day— this is very difficult for me."

"I understand."

"It means looking back. Accepting the loss."

Muriel examined the haggard features, the dark fractured gaze, and guessed, "There was a woman?"

He nodded slowly. "And a child. A baby girl. I lost them both to the influenza."

"What were their names?"

"Sarah. And Gabrielle."

"I shall pray for them," she said. "And for you."

: CHAPTER 9 :

:

The next day was divided in two. In the morning, Muriel arose from her narrow bed, alive and eager. She dressed in the clothes she had brought with her from America. They seemed drab now in comparison to the city that surrounded her. But they were familiar, and they permitted her to withdraw from the center of attention, to disappear in plain view. Which was how she had always gone through life, Muriel realized. Photography fit her like a glove sewn for her own hand. She was most comfortable standing apart and watching from a safe distance. Here she was, for the first time in her life, caught up in the world's affairs, and still she was happiest when she could place the camera between her and events.

She saw people more clearly when she was framing them in terms of space and light and shadow. She connected with them most intimately when viewing them through the lens. The camera was not merely a window. It was the way through which she could open her heart.

Often she found herself thinking back to the moment when the reliquary was opened and the fragment revealed. She lifted the camera to capture a mother and daughter laughing over a balloon, and saw instead the Greek letters carved into the case. At such times, she would touch the cross hanging from her neck, feel the smooth olive wood, and sense a greater Presence, a true bonding with the world beyond this world.

After a lunch taken in a street-side café, Muriel returned to her room to find a note waiting for her from Senator Bryan. It was written on embassy stationery in a hand she assumed was not his own, with feminine flourishes and no signature. She was instructed to meet him at four at the ambassador's residence. At the bottom were two additional words: *Dress appropriately.*

Muriel went upstairs and unpacked the boxes from Chanel, hanging them in her narrow cupboard and fingering the fabric. The colors were muted, one ivory with a hint of tan, the other a pale grayish blue. Both were made from a new fabric called muslin. Muriel had read about the cloth and the style in magazines she had never shown her mother. The dresses were both daring and extremely conservative. The hems reached her shoes, the small pearl buttons rose almost to her chin. Yet they were cut so as to accentuate her femininity. Muriel dressed and did her hair and face in the style she had been shown, then stood before the oval mirror, trying to claim this stranger as herself.

The United States ambassador's residence stood on the Rue Françoise in the first arrondissement. During the war, it had served as the headquarters for America's charitable relief efforts. Muriel thought the formal salons were beautiful. Tea was served in the smallest of four audience chambers, a wood-lined alcove that comfortably held the two dozen guests. Senator Bryan arrived with the ambassador, a grandfatherly figure to whom Muriel felt instantly drawn.

On the surface, it was a pleasant affair. But the afternoon

was disrupted by Maurice Maunoury, minister of the interior and Charles Fouchet's superior. Muriel had merely glimpsed the minister at the prime minister's reception. At the ambassador's residence, she could not escape him. Minister Maunoury proved to be an intensely cold man with a wandering eye. He captured her in the alcove by the fireplace and demanded to know what her plans were.

"My plans," she replied, "are to serve the senator as he requests."

"How nice." He turned the words into a slur. "Let us hope the senator deserves such allegiance."

"He does, Sir. Most certainly."

"And if the senator intends to take you into harm's way?"

"That will not happen, Sir."

He sniffed. "Where are you headed from Paris?"

"I have not been informed."

"I have heard the city of Constantinople being mentioned." He crowded her further into the corner. "It is a perilous city at the best of times."

"May I ask what business this is of yours?"

"No, you may not." He reached toward her. "What a charming frock."

"If you will excuse me, Sir—"

"I have not dismissed you," he snapped.

"I am not yours to dismiss. Now excuse me!" Muriel used volume to push the man away. When that did not work, she ducked down and slipped away from him.

Charles Fouchet found her fuming by the windows overlooking the rear garden. "Is everything all right?"

"How can you stand to work for that man?"

"He and my father were at school together. His son and I were the closest of friends. He has offered me a chance most men could never dream of having." He studied her. "The minister said something inappropriate?"

"He…" She decided there was nothing to be gained by criticizing his sponsor. "He said we were going to Constantinople."

Charles sighed. "That was not his news to share."

"So it's true."

"It is what I have heard. I'm sorry, I am most reluctant to discuss rumors."

"Why did he mention it?"

"The minister of the interior is also responsible for the police and the state's internal security forces." He spoke very carefully. "The position carries with it the power of holding secrets."

"I don't understand."

Charles studied her with frank admiration. "No, and that is one of your most endearing traits."

She felt warmed by his gaze. "I don't know what you are talking about, but thank you just the same."

"Would you care for more tea?"

"In a minute. Can I please share with you a secret of my own?"

"I would count it a great honor."

"Perhaps it is nothing. But I think I am being followed."

He tensed. "What makes you say that?"

"A man keeps showing up. Only for an instant, then vanishing."

"When did this happen?"

"The first time was when we emerged from Saint Denis. I

noticed him because he was so different from the others around us. Their faces were filled with the sense of peace and joy. His…"

"Describe him."

She was tempted to say, "He looked just like you do now. Cold and as focused as a rifle barrel." But instead, she described, "Not as tall as you. Narrow features, dark clothes. Gloves. That was another thing. The afternoon was warm, and he was the only man wearing gloves that I noticed. And a hat, a narrow-brimmed homburg, slate gray with a black ribbon. Very hard eyes. He stared straight at me, then turned away and vanished."

"So you saw him only briefly."

"One glance and then he was gone."

"Yet you observed with a photographer's eye for details. When did he next appear?"

"Outside Notre Dame. I saw him when we left the stalls and walked toward the taxis. And then today. I think. He vanished inside a shop. If it was him."

He reached for her arm. "We must tell the ambassador."

"No, please. What if I'm wrong, and it was nothing?"

He looked at her, and she saw then the other man he was. The soldier, the warrior, the survivor. All he said was, "Come."

• • •

The next morning when Muriel came downstairs, she discovered Charles Fouchet there waiting for her. He bowed stiffly and announced, "I am instructed to accompany you."

"You couldn't possibly."

"It would either be me or a guard who neither knows you nor cares."

Muriel felt her face grow warm. "Then let it be a guard."

Charles frowned. "Do you mean that truly?"

"All this makes me out to be far more important than I am. You are the minister's private secretary—"

"And the minister has instructed me to accompany you to Constantinople."

"I couldn't ask....What?"

"This morning, the senator's journey was officially confirmed and the minister has ordered me to go, to see, and to report."

"I don't understand."

"Nor do I. But one thing I can tell you for certain, Miss Muriel. There is more at stake in the French government's eyes than a reliquary. Even if this one is real."

She felt eyes upon them from every corner of the hotel lobby and the adjoining restaurant. "What am I supposed to do?"

He indicated the sunlit world beyond the entrance. "I am not here to dictate a schedule. The day is yours until you meet the senator at four this afternoon. I am merely to escort."

"So the man I saw..."

"Might or might not have been an adversary. But everyone agrees it is a chance we cannot take."

She felt a small thrill. "I did not mean to suggest that I wasn't happy to see you, Monsieur."

"Please, now that we are to be companions upon the road, I must insist you call me Charles."

"Since you are coming, would you mind helping me with my equipment?"

He truly had the loveliest smile. "I should be honored to serve as your willing beast of burden."

They traveled to one of the oldest of the many bridges linking the two banks of Paris. The Pont des Invalides had originally been set in place by the Romans, who treated the city as a warehouse for the fodder grown in the verdant Seine pasturelands. The bridge was slightly humped, so it rose and fell like a stone hill above the city's flowing heart. With the sun behind her, Muriel set up the tripod and the Graflex camera where the bridge joined the broad promenade. She fastened the cloak into place so that she could vanish. The pedestrians crossing the bridge toward her faced the sun, making it difficult to see the camera in any case. The sky was perfect, a pleasant mix of cloud and sun, light and shadow. The other side of the river was decorated by mansard roofs and church spires. She raised the tripod as far as it would go, but she still needed to bend over to frame the shots. Her back was beginning to ache when she heard a voice from beyond the cloak say, "Here, Muriel. Sit."

She lifted the cloak to discover a stool standing beside her. "Where did this come from?"

"The café across the street. The proprietor asks only that you come and take a photograph of his wife when you are done."

"Thank you!" She retreated back behind the cloak and gave herself over to the joy of taking pictures.

The idea had come to her late at night, the way to photograph the people so that the city became a component of their character. The Seine was more than a liquid divider between the Left and Right Banks. It was the magnet that drew the populace. They came and they strolled and they shopped and they bonded with the city's nucleus. The river barges chugged past, drawing the attention of the children and their mothers. Muriel captured one shot after another, revealing the vivid emotions of people who thought their lives went unnoticed.

A mother stood by the railing with a pair of young girls who laughed joyfully at a boat passing beneath their feet. The mother's face created a portrait of contrasts, for she looked at her children with a sadness so complete she did not need to cry.

A pair of young lovers embraced, framed by an elderly couple who smiled in wistful remembrance as the lady laid her husband's hand upon her withered cheek.

A young boy danced into view, playing a game all his own with the balloon he held, while his mother laughed and called and tried to catch hold of the human balloon who danced just out of reach.

A pair of shopgirls came into view, walking arm in arm. They caught sight of Charles and began a flirtatious dance. But Charles did not see them. It did not appear that Charles saw anything at all. Muriel captured the moment the girls threw back their heads and dismissed him with shared laughter.

And then she focused upon Charles.

Like all professional cameras, the Graflex showed the photographer a precise replica of what the lens captured. The rear image was the exact size of the photographic negative, only it was upside down. Professional photographers learned to right the view in their mind's eye.

Charles had seated himself on one of the stone benches lining the bridge. He faced across the bridge so that he could keep an eye on everyone who passed—only Charles was not watching the pedestrians or the street. His vision was clouded by some distant memory, one so powerful he had aged twenty years, thirty, a hundred. He bore the flinty countenance of a man forced to endure things that no human should ever know.

Muriel took his picture. Then she stopped in the process of

changing the negative plate and slipped from beneath the cloak. Charles showed no awareness as she left the camera and walked over. She seated herself beside him, hesitated, then reached over and took his hand. Charles turned toward her, but it seemed to Muriel that he did not actually recognize her.

He took a deep breath, blinked, drew the world into focus. Breathed again. "I was...away."

"I understand."

"My life since the Armistice has been..."

"Frantic."

"Desperately so. And I want it that way. But now, I was thinking...I was not there when they buried my wife and daughter. The news missed me in Verdun and again at the base where I was decommissioned, and then I returned home, and..."

"I'm so sorry."

"I could not bring myself to go to their graves. For a week, I puttered about our home. And then one night I woke up and found myself wanting to set the place alight, burn it down with me inside it. And I knew if I stayed, I would perish. So I forced myself to the cemetery at dawn, said my farewells, and came here, only to discover the minister had been looking for me as well. Since then, I have been running. I have volunteered for every duty, no matter how small. This is the first time I have allowed myself to stop, to think, to..."

Muriel was still searching for the proper words when she saw him.

"Charles."

"I must apologize for disturbing you with such—"

"I see him."

"Eh, what?"

"The man who followed me. He's here."

Charles made no motion. His gaze remained directed at the river and the boats. But Muriel felt him tense. The hand she held turned as hard and cold as his voice. "Don't stare."

"I spotted him and instantly turned away."

"Good. Now tell me precisely where he is."

"The café across the street. He is standing to the right, so the shadow of the awning hides him."

"But you're certain it was him?"

"He shifted and drew into the light. That was when I noticed him." She found herself shivering. "It is the same man."

Charles rose slowly, turned, and smiled down at her as he released her hand. Taking his ease. Only the hard cast to his features revealed the transformation. "Wait here."

She dared not breathe for a long moment after he left. The day's colors faded, the people no longer held her. She stared at the cloud-flecked sky and the sparkling waters and the passing boats. But all she saw was the whirl of mystery.

Charles returned and slipped onto the bench beside her. "He's gone."

CHAPTER 10

That evening, Muriel dressed in her fine Chanel gown and descended the central stairs to the hotel lounge. Charles Fouchet was there waiting for her, his dove-gray formal cutaway as stern and striking as a general's uniform. He bowed at her arrival and escorted her outside, where the elderly porter greeted her formally and held open the carriage door.

They traveled the short distance to the Place de l'Opéra, where they joined the long line of carriages waiting to deposit their charges. Muriel said, "Can we walk?"

"But of course."

The evening was cool and the air filled with fragrances from the neighboring vegetable market. The stallholders paused in their sweeping and dismantling to watch Muriel and Charles pass. Muriel felt separated from them in a way that was far from pleasant. When she photographed, she felt as though she was creating a portal through which she could observe and bond and remain safe. This isolation of luxury did not suit her.

The opera house's palatial foyer was a swirling mass of gay chatter and brilliant colors. Muriel felt eyes on her as she passed, and forced herself to walk as she recalled Madame Chanel had done, with shoulders back and eyes aimed at the horizon. The ambassador saw her first and pointed the senator around. He gave a stiff little bow and kissed her hand. "My dear, you look ravishing."

"Thank you, Sir. But you have seen the dress twice before, at the boutique and again at the reception."

"Before, you wore a dress that was not yours," he replied. "Tonight you inhabit it."

She mulled that over as introductions were made around the large group. When the ambassador came to Minister Maunoury, Charles's superior, he waved his cigar at her and said, "Welcome to the fold, Mademoiselle."

"Monsieur?"

"You are being watched!" He boomed the words with false cheeriness. "It is the price of power. One of them. To be constantly under observation by the enemy."

She found herself chilled. "I hold no power of any kind, Minister."

"Obviously there are those who disagree. And in the Great Game, appearances are all that matter!"

Senator Bryan saw both her distress and the ambassador's frown and demanded, "What is he saying?"

As she started to respond, Muriel caught a hard glint to the minister's eye. She was certain the man spoke English. And that his words had been directed at the senator all along. Muriel said, "The minister is simply making polite conversation, Senator."

The minister hid his displeasure by puffing intently on his cigar. The rising smoke tightened the folds of fat about Minister Maunoury's eyes into slits. Then Muriel caught the ambassador watching her.

He nodded his approval, then said, "Shall we find our seats?"

Porters in gilded uniforms ushered their group into a box that hung over the stage. Muriel was seated on the front row between the ambassador and the senator. While the others settled, Senator Bryan murmured, "Tell me what the minister said."

When Muriel had finished relating the exchange, Senator Bryan said, "He was warning me."

"I assumed that was the case. But why?"

"France stands against us on all the issues related to Constantinople. I have been meeting with various officials to explain that our position would in fact benefit their government. My efforts have done little good."

"Are we in danger?"

"Absolutely not. Harming us would only weaken their position."

"Then why—"

"They do not want us traveling to Turkey. They assume the connections that have opened up because of our hunt for the reliquary are in truth a disguise for subterfuge and influence peddling. It is what the French would do. It is what they are best at."

Muriel stared out over the audience, wondering at the multitude of issues which she did not understand. "So when the prime minister supported my viewing the reliquary at Notre Dame…"

"He was going against members of his own government who suspect that whatever we claim to be doing in Constantinople is only a cover for our real objective, which is to thwart France's claims over the Dardanelles."

"Is any of that true?"

"I am formally charged by the president to present our government's position to the rulers in Constantinople. I am also directed to take a measure of the situation." He fumed quietly, his voice thick with frustration. "There are those in our government who would like nothing more than to enter into direct conflict with the French. I consider them foolhardy. One does not build alliances by taking advantage of temporary weaknesses. The French are a proud and ancient nation with strong historical ties to America. We should be helping to rebuild them and striving to convince them that our position is the right one." He glanced over. "Do I bore you?"

"Quite the contrary, Senator. I am honored that you would confide in me."

He returned his stony gaze to the empty stage. "My enemies consider me soft and addled both. They consider my quest to be misguided. They call me Don Quixote with a cross. I hold my tongue. I do not respond. I let them think what they will. I have done this all my life. But I will share the truth with you, Miss Muriel. I feel called by my Lord to this duty."

She felt a hundred questions press at her heart, but the conductor was entering the orchestra pit and the audience was applauding, and she knew she would have to wait for answers. "Thank you for trusting me, Senator."

He applauded with the others and said with fierce vehemence, "I know you will not let me down."

: CHAPTER 11 :

:

After a morning taking pictures at the world-famous market of Les Halles, Muriel and Charles traveled to the American Embassy on the corner of the Avenue Marceau and the Rue Galilée. A Marine guard escorted Muriel into the building and up to the second floor. Senator Bryan had taken over what clearly had been an aide's office, just across the hall from the ambassador's formal chambers. He rose from his desk, closed the file he had been working on, and asked if she would like tea. When she refused, he reseated himself and said, "Charles informs me that you have been told of our travel plans."

"About Constantinople, yes."

"I never had any intention of keeping you in the dark. But I only received the formal invitation to travel this morning. Might I ask how you heard?"

"From Minister Maunoury. He mentioned it at the ambassador's reception."

The senator winced. "What precisely did the minister say?"

As Muriel related the exchange, the senator tapped his fingers lightly on the desk's leather top. "I had suspected all along that factions within the French regime were seeking to thwart my aims."

"He said nothing about that."

"Not directly. But the French are masters at inferences. It grants them the ability to deny everything later, if it suits them."

"Why would he be opposed to your seeking a reliquary?"

"Because…" Senator Bryan stopped at a knock on his door. "Come in."

A young man dressed in the formal black cutaway coat required of all staffers announced, "Your call has come through, Sir."

"Splendid." He rose and beckoned Muriel to join him. "Come with me."

The young man led them down the hall and up the stairs at a trot. Muriel did not have the breath to either protest or ask where they were going. They were led into a windowless chamber on the first floor, where a young man was seated at a telegraph. When they entered, he announced, "We are ready at this end."

The senator said, "Be brief, my dear."

Muriel settled onto the stool behind the telegraph operator, who listened intently to the ticking machine, and made swift notes on his pad. He then read, "Hello, Muriel, my dear. We are missing you so very much. The weather has been glorious. Everyone at church has been asking about you. When are you coming home?"

Never had the distance separating Muriel from her home felt as vast as now, seated on that uncomfortable stool, listening to the man drone her mother's words.

The telegraph operator asked, "Do you wish to respond?"

Murel swallowed hard, and replied, "Very soon. I love you both so much."

The young man tapped the key with impossible swiftness. Then he retrieved his pencil when the machine began clicking in reply. He read, "Daughter, Thomas has indicated that you might be traveling further afield. You have our blessing."

Only her father referred to Muriel in that fashion. She swiped impatiently at her cheeks and said, "Thank you, Daddy. I'm taking some wonderful pictures."

This time, the repsonse from across the ocean took much longer. When the machine went silent, the telegraph operator read, "I was always certain the world would one day hear of my daughter, the photographer and historian. But I ask you to promise that they will also hear of you, the believer. Know we pray for you. Take care, darling."

: CHAPTER 12 :

:

That afternoon she traveled to the photographic studio responsible for developing her photographs. The studio had come highly recommended, both by Charles Fouchet and someone on the ambassador's staff. Even so, Muriel entered the shop with her heart in her mouth. So much depended upon the people and their work. Not to mention her own abilities as a photographer.

As she stood at the counter and waited for the shopkeeper to sort through his manila envelopes of prints, Muriel felt her heart hammer in her throat. She had known such nerves on any number of occasions, agonizing over the doubts and worries, uncertain of her abilities and her equipment and the day and...

"Here they are, Mademoiselle." The man was small and graying and had pianist's hands, with long, supple fingers that were stained by years of development chemicals. He slid the four packets across the counter and smiled as she unwrapped the twine seals with trembling fingers.

She knew she should probably view them in the privacy of her hotel room, but she could not wait. Charles stood at a discreet distance as she spilled first one envelope and then another onto the counter.

Normally, a photographer would ask for the negatives to be developed, then examine them and decide which should be made into prints. But Senator Bryan had repeatedly told her that time was of the essence and cost was a secondary issue. So for the first time in her life, Muriel had the opportunity to view as a print every single photograph she had taken. What was more, the development had been done by a professional. Muriel was certain of this the instant she saw the first pictures.

The first packet contained those taken of the reliquary. Muriel breathed a huge sigh of relief as she studied each in turn. They were precise, the lighting perfect, the details very clear. She could even see the grain in the wood, the fold of the silver around the corners, the way the letters had been carved. Muriel asked for a magnifying loupe, examined them for a time, and knew the senator would be pleased.

Another customer came into the shop, and the manager moved down the counter so as to separate this activity from her. Muriel took the opportunity to spread out her pictures from the Paris streets. Senator Bryan had insisted upon her taking the same liberty with her own work as the church pictures. She reveled in the chance to scrutinize each shot. Especially the mistakes. There were errors in positioning and background that she would never have noticed through looking only at negatives. She had long wanted her own studio, but her mother's allergies made it impossible to have the chemicals in their home. Gradually Muriel began sorting out the photographs that were worth keeping. More customers came and went. Time passed. She adjusted the photographs' positions to catch the sunlight as it progressed across the sky.

Finally, the manager came back and inspected with her. Charles took that as his long-awaited sign and stepped forward. "May I see?"

"Mademoiselle has taken a remarkable picture here," the manager said.

"The street sweeper," Charles said. "A war veteran."

"So I was told," Muriel said, resisting the sudden urge to trace his vacant face with her finger.

"So mademoiselle is aware of this? And how wonderfully she has managed to convey the shadows in his eyes." The manager plucked the loupe from her hand and bent over the photograph. "Look here, the light catches the water as he cleans the street and reflects him. Did the mademoiselle know the reflection made his greatcoat look like a tattered uniform?"

Suddenly she could no longer focus upon the picture. She sensed as much as saw how Charles leaned closer still. "You are right, Monsieur."

"Of course I am." The manager turned to the next picture. "And this one of the three children, *magnifique*."

Charles shifted the pictures then froze. "This woman..."

"*Regardez*. The tragedy of war, there upon her face." The manager leaned in so close he blocked Muriel's view. He was almost cheek-to-cheek beside Charles. "Perhaps she sees the father and husband, a man she no doubt lost to the war, there in the face of these young ones, yes?"

Charles took a ragged breath. He swallowed hard and stepped away to stand by the door, staring out of the shop. Isolated and alone.

The manager gently tapped the photographs back together,

refit them into the envelope, and handed them over with a sad and gentle smile. "Mademoiselle has an artist's eye."

: CHAPTER 13 :
:

T hat night they took the Orient Express.

The train had been withdrawn from service six years earlier, when passage through the eastern reaches had become dangerous. The carriages smelled faintly of camphor and oil and disuse. Muriel did not care. The Orient Express was the most elegant train ever created, with rosewood paneling and gilded ceilings and velvet drapes and plush carpets and crystal chandeliers in the public carriages.

Her chamber was a jewel box of precise elegance, tiny and beautiful. She shared a butler with five other cabins, an elderly gentleman who carried himself with the smiling formality of a favorite grandfather. Muriel adored him on sight. She loved everything about the trip. She was in heaven before the train left the station.

Charles Fouchet traveled in the coach behind the one where she and Senator Bryan had their rooms. An hour after crossing the Seine, the three of them gathered in the dining car. Charles and Senator Bryan wore formal evening wear and she her dark blue gown. After dinner, she returned to her cabin, feeling as though she danced along the swaying corridor, buoyed by dreams that were finally coming true.

Muriel had no idea how long she had been asleep when the dream came to her. She was drawn into a mist-bound realm by the sound of a vast choir, as though the entire world both spoke and chanted the words. Gradually the words became clear to her, and when they did, she saw for the first time where she had arrived.

She was alone in a church. It was shaped like Notre Dame, yet so large the ceiling was lost to drifting clouds. The vast chamber echoed to a refrain chanted by thousands of unseen voices: *Lamb of God, who takes away the sins of the world.*

There upon the altar was the reliquary. She felt it call to her, a magnet designed to entice her heart. She floated up the central aisle, much as she had along the train's hallway. She was supported and urged on by the voices. The melodious chant grew louder the closer she came to the front table. *Lamb of God.*

The reliquary grew larger as she approached. The gold faded. The filigree and the beauty and the shimmering jewels all vanished. Until there was nothing there before her but the wood.

And yet the closer she came, the more glorious became the sight. She felt a weight upon her that was as old as the human race, chains that gripped her and tried to hold her back. And still the voices chanted and carried her forward, until finally she stood upon the rocky earth, and there before her rose the cross. It towered up into a dark and stormy sky, and she wept with the knowledge that Christ's tragic hour had been caused by her own impossible need.

She reached out to touch the wood. And in that instant, she came awake. She was sobbing so hard she could scarcely draw breath. Her right hand gripped the simple wooden cross that hung around her neck.

Muriel slid to the train's floor and knelt, her hands clasped on the bed. She was filled with the dread of coming challenge. Beyond the luxury and the rumbling journey, Muriel sensed a great moment ahead. She felt as though she had been preparing for this all her life. God had called her. Of that she had no doubt. She was still there on her knees when dawn filled her cabin with new light.

· · ·

When she came into the dining car that early morning, Senator Bryan was the only other customer. He was so intent upon the book open by his plate that he did not notice her. She started to pass his table but then realized he was studying the Scriptures. "May I join you?"

He looked up, saw that she carried her own Bible, and replied, "I would be delighted."

They studied for a time in silence. Then Senator Bryan said, "I have been looking forward to this journey. Not the destination. The trip itself. I have such little time to myself these days."

"You have been so busy."

"Not just busy. I have been assaulted on all sides. I needed time to commune and reflect."

"I can move to another table if you—"

"I wouldn't think of it. You are as easy on the soul as you are on the eyes." He leaned back as the waiter refilled his coffee cup, then mused to the early light beyond the window, "I have been sitting here looking at the same passage for well over an hour and thinking about my early life. My father was a wealthy industrialist. I was the fourth child, all boys. We admired our father above all living men. He steered me into the law and then into a Washington firm, the goal of political office never far from my father's mind. I never thought of rebellion. I did as I was told. But now as I approach my own final hour, I find myself wondering about it all. My children are grown, and my wife I lost six years ago in the epidemic's early days, back before we knew what it was."

"Have you ever thought of remarrying?"

"The question is put to me by every socialite in Washington. I tell them that in time, perhaps. But in truth, I have no interest in anyone. I miss Anabelle too much."

She studied the man seated across from her. The lone waiter stood at the car's far end, leaning against the bar, idly polishing a glass. It was as close to a private moment as she had known with Thomas Bryan. "I envy you that love," she confessed. "My parents have this as well, the closeness that goes beyond the moment or the hour. I cannot imagine one of them without the other."

"Your parents are the salt of the earth, and you are a credit to them both."

"My mother does not understand my yearning for more than what she has."

"She is the product of another time. Even so, she accepts your need for your own course."

"Very, very reluctantly," Muriel said.

The senator smiled. "When your father agreed to your joining me on this quest, she did not object."

On an impulse, she rose from her chair. "Will you excuse me for a moment?"

She returned down the rocking carriages to her cabin, opened her case, and pulled out the manila envelope containing her portfolio of pictures. She carried them back to the dining car and set it down in front of the senator. "I thought you might like to see what I have been doing."

He undid the velvet ribbon and opened the top. The first images were the best of those from the church. Muriel had already supplied him with copies. Even so, he went through them slowly. He had experience in handling a professional's work, touching only the edge of each picture, lifting them by a fingernail and setting them carefully to one side. When he arrived at her portraits, he slowed further. Several times, he paused in utter stillness, his hand hovering to the side of the photograph. He did not speak until the final picture had been examined. He turned it facedown and rested his fingers upon the back. When he looked up, his eyes were wet. "Is that all?"

"All that I am satisfied with."

"My dear, these are...magnificent. You have a gift."

Only then did Muriel realize she had been holding her breath. "Thank you."

"Do you know why the premier was willing to help you? It was because of your compassionate heart and your ability to perceive what most people miss. These same attributes are what make your photographs unique. You must be careful with this gift, my dear. The world is often unkind to the openhearted among us."

"I-I don't understand. Is that a warning?"

He gathered up the photographs, tapped them into order, and settled them back into the folder. His movements were measured, as cautious as his words. "I suspect you are growing fond of Charles Fouchet."

She watched his hands and searched for some response. But none came to mind.

"You know of his loss, the wife and child?"

"I...Yes. He told me."

"If I were your father, which I am not, but if I were, I would warn you that some men cannot be healed by a good woman's love. No matter how much you might wish things to be otherwise."

She forced herself to reply, "With God all things are possible."

"True." The smile he offered her was infinitely sad. "But for that to happen, the individual must himself pray for the miracle. Some men fear that such a healing will mean losing the final fragment of their former love. I know this must be hard for you to understand. You are fresh and young and filled with the promise of unseen days."

He turned to the window, and Muriel realized he was lost to her now. His gaze held the light of both sorrow and yearning as he looked beyond the morning to a time that was no more. He said softly, "God may heal, and yet he may also offer an alternative. One that is difficult to fathom, but real nonetheless. To walk alone, and yet comforted by the knowledge that another waits patiently, beyond the final door."

He glanced over and seemed to find it difficult to place her. He blinked once, again, and forced himself to smile. "If Charles is such a man, my dear, his choices may take him in directions that you would be well advised not to follow."

: CHAPTER 14 :

:

They arrived in Venice at mid-morning, where they had a seven-hour stop. The train station was on the mainland, directly opposite the water-bound city. The three of them took a gondola to the Grand Canal. The senator was polished and polite to Charles, who responded with the easy charm of a professional diplomat. But Muriel sensed an edge to their conversation and wondered if it had been there all along. Or if perhaps it was the journey itself that caused a new boundary. Or, worse still, if she caused this herself.

They dined at the Danieli, the city's oldest hotel, in a restaurant fashioned from a floating veranda as large as a ballroom. The strong Mediterranean sunlight was filtered through a striped canopy. The waters lapped on the stone landing below their table. A pair of gondoliers rowed past, singing in harmony as they plied the waters. Three swans swooped in for a landing beyond the docks, their wings making sweet music in the still air. It was as beautiful a setting as Muriel had ever imagined, and she wished for the ability to shut out her unwelcome thoughts and give herself fully to the day.

After lunch, Charles offered to take her to Saint Mark's Square. The senator declined their invitation to join them. They strolled down one idyllic lane after another, with sunlight and pigeons and tourists and locals for companions. Finally, Charles asked, "Will you tell me what is troubling you?"

Muriel decided she could not share the senator's comments. Not directly. Not without confessing her own feelings. Which she most definitely was not willing to do. "What causes the tension between you and the senator?"

"It is not between us, but rather our governments." He formed two fists and planted them before his face. "South of Constantinople is one of the world's busiest waterways. It is the only link between the Black Sea and Europe. This controls Russia's only access to the Mediterranean and her only ports that do not ice over in winter. Whoever controls the Dardanelles Strait controls Asia."

"But France and America are allies."

"Not when it comes to the strait." Charles dropped his hands. "France has been ally of the Ottoman caliphs for three hundred years. America calls them corrupt and decadent, which they most certainly are. France has helped prop up the empire; America wants them replaced by a democracy."

She felt the chill dread of past hardships rise up with his words. "Will there be war?"

He frowned at the sky above the cathedral's dome. "I pray not."

"But you fear yes?"

"Many of France's strongest remaining industries rely on trade with the Ottoman Empire. If it falls, they fall. Or so they claim. France resents America's meddling in what she considers her own back yard."

"Why are you here?"

"Two reasons. First, to assess the situation. I know war. The minister is fed up with the reports the embassy is sending and wants a fresh perspective from a man with military training."

"And second?" When he did not respond, she pressed, "To spy on us?"

"So long as the senator does what he says, which is find his artifact and study the situation as I will, we have no conflict."

"But your superiors think otherwise?"

"They do." He looked at her, his expression grave. "I hope and pray they are wrong."

• • •

The next two days rattled and hummed along. They gathered for meals. Mornings, Muriel joined the senator for a time of quiet study. They rarely spoke in these periods, and if they did, it was of her family. Their destination was left for a future that was comfortably beyond the next sunset and the next dawn.

Occasionally, Muriel found the two men seated together, talking in grave tones that left her feeling excluded. She retreated unseen.

She spent many hours alone, either in her cabin or in the carriage fitted out as a formal parlor. She found herself reveling in such periods. The vistas outside her windows were ever changing, great flat fields beneath gray skies, tilled by people and oxen and donkeys in a fashion that looked unchanged for centuries beyond count. Mountains drifted in the distance, the color of slate, uninviting and grim. Then the sun reappeared, and the world was transformed to a place of hope and promise. Water sparkled in the distance, rivers and tributaries that flowed into the unseen Mediterranean. Sails drifted down broad rivers, fishing nets flashed, and Muriel wished the journey would never end.

They arrived in Constantinople at daybreak. The city bustled and beckoned. Minarets rose like a man-made forest, steep pinnacles that pierced the new day. The city was one great, confusing roar. Donkeys brayed, hawkers yelled, people rushed. The senator and Muriel stood by their luggage while Charles went in search of a carriage. Passersby cast Muriel dark, unreadable glances and moved on. Beggars clustered and pleaded.

Charles returned with a carriage and two porters, who waved away the screeching beggars and loaded their luggage in a rush of strong arms and calls in a foreign tongue. The beggars wailed as she climbed into the carriage, but none dared touch the foreign lady. Muriel pushed down the sliding window and leaned out. The alienness of Constantinople surrounded her on all sides. Beyond the crowded avenue rose a humpbacked bridge where men fished with long poles. Their catches sparkled and danced in the sunlight. On the bridge's other side rose another forest of minarets. Muriel took a deep breath and felt her heart surge with the excitement of being here, of being alive.

The city was both crumbling and full of life, as though the people thrived on the decay and the tumult and the din. The journey to the American embassy took over an hour. Soon as the carriage halted, another herd of beggars rushed up. The driver and his young assistant shouted and drove them back with staves and were soon joined by two soldiers in khaki uniforms and puttees. Muriel was ushered through rusting gates and entered another world.

Charles came up to stand beside her. "This is how life is throughout the Orient. Chaos outside the walls, wonder within."

"You have traveled here often?"

"Once only to Constantinople. The last journey my father took before the war. But I have lived all over. My family was always on the move..."

He stopped because a man in the formal striped trousers and cutaway coat of the diplomatic service rushed forward. "Senator Bryan, forgive me, your cable arrived only this morning. I sent my own carriage, but I see it did not arrive in time."

"Think nothing of it." He ushered Muriel forward. "May I have the pleasure of introducing my associate from the Smithsonian, Muriel Ross. My dear, this is Ambassador Eveland Holland, legate to the Ottoman court."

He was a slender man in his sixties, with an angular nose over a salt-and-pepper moustache. Two unruly wisps of silver hair clung to either side of an utterly bald head. He looked to Muriel like a worried stork. The hand he offered her was moist and limp. She resisted the urge to wipe her fingers on her skirt. "I am honored, sir."

"I wish I could say the same." The ambassador scarcely glanced her way. "Senator—"

"And this is Charles Fouchet, personal attaché to Minister Maunoury."

The ambassador looked askance. "You are traveling with a member of the French government?"

"I am, and I would be grateful if you would find accommodation for him as well."

The ambassador's mouth opened several times before he said, "Sir, forgive me, but surely the gentleman would be more comfortable at his own legation."

"No doubt. But I wish for him to remain here." Senator Bryan's smile turned steely. "With us."

"Very well, Senator. But I must tell you, if I had known you were even considering such a journey, I would have protested in the strongest possible terms."

"The president himself approved my voyage. He requested it, in fact."

"Then, Sir, I would have protested to him as well. With respect, there is no way anyone in Washington could possibly understand what is happening here." The ambassador waved a hand at the gates, where the two soldiers were once again standing guard. "Outside these walls is a city waiting to ignite. I cannot stress too highly the danger we face. Tonight could very well be our last."

: CHAPTER 15 :
:

Muriel's bedchamber was on the legation's top floor, in what had once been the servant's lodgings. The room was long and narrow and had three cat's-eye windows that extended over the eaves. The scarred floor held shadows where once six beds and tables had stood. But it was all hers, and the view was stupendous. She hung up her clothes in the wardrobe, bathed, and dressed in one of the more modest dresses she had brought from home. She spent the hour before lunch seated by the central window, staring out over the city, yearning to go out and look and absorb and experience.

At midday, a man in a fez and white apron walked through the central courtyard below, striking a xylophone he held in one arm. Muriel descended the stairs and joined the chattering flow into the main dining room. The ground-floor rooms were very grand, with frescoed ceilings and gilded bas-relief pillars. Muriel was stared at, but no one spoke to her. She had known such treatment from her early days at the Smithsonian, when the other researchers had taken acidic pleasure in pretending she was invisible. She was too young, she was too inexperienced, and she was too eager to learn and grow and move on. Muriel had remained determined to never become mummified like them.

And now here she was again. She had traveled halfway around the world to experience the same petty spite. She sat alone at a table by the far wall, eating food she did not taste, surrounded by other people who had developed the professional ability to exclude, to ignore.

"May I join you?"

She greeted Charles Fouchet with a smile from the heart. "I have been trying to tell myself that I do not mind being alone."

"The ambassador has protested to the senator over your presence. These embassy officials are professionals at reading the political winds." He nodded his thanks as a waiter placed a plate down in front of him. "What are we eating?"

"Boiled beef. At least, I think it's beef."

"That is the problem with the Orient. When Westerners insist upon being served food they find familiar, the local cooks are both baffled and insulted." He took a bite and grimaced. "This is dreadful."

"I agree."

"This will not do." He set his napkin to one side and rose from the table. "Excuse me."

Muriel watched him cross the room, a leopard drifting through a crowd of mice. Charles Fouchet was not handsome in any conventional sense. His features were too severe, and the scar that ran down the left side of his face was a jarring reminder of whatever had shattered his dark gaze. But his was a commanding presence, and Muriel liked him. Then she recalled the senator's warning, and her insides went cold with a sudden wash of fear. Even so, her feelings could not be denied. Her affections for Charles grew with each meeting.

He returned from the kitchen, followed by two beaming waiters. They swept up the two plates and deposited new ones in their place. The food was very odd-looking, particularly the meat, which was ground and then shaped like a cigar. The smell was spectacular. "What is this?"

One of the waiters replied, "Döner kebab, honored Mistress. Named for my city. Very good. Turkish food. You try."

She took a bite and proclaimed, "Marvelous!"

Both waiters smiled broadly. "Turkish food, it is best in world, you see."

Charles said, "I asked for plates of whatever they were having."

The rice was unlike any she had ever seen, colored like dirty dishwater and filled with what appeared to be chopped leaves. But the flavor was exquisite. Midway through the meal, Muriel was suddenly caught by an urge to share her secret with Charles. Perhaps it was the way the rest of the room pointedly ignored them. Maybe it was the easy silence, or the way he had transformed the meal from an ordeal into a delight. Whatever the reason, as soon as she started speaking, she knew it was the right thing to do.

She told him about the dream and the sense of coming close to the center of salvation. The weeping, and the hours she spent on her knees afterward. Midway through the description, Charles pushed his plate to one side and leaned his chin against his fists. He watched her in brooding silence, his gaze as open and dark as a tomb.

When she was done, he took a long time responding. "I once knew such a faith. A confidence that the day would be fine and the Lord of all was with me."

"He was, and he is," she said softly.

Charles breathed in and out, great heaves of his chest that left her feeling as though inside where no one could see, the man wept. "It is nice that you still think so. But this world has shown me such things…"

"I cannot imagine what you have endured," she said. "But I do know that God is still there for you. Waiting. Ready to heal. And offer you a tomorrow."

"I have a tomorrow, thanks to Minister Maunoury."

Muriel did not respond.

"Yes, yes, he can be difficult at times. But most men of power develop such sharp edges. It is the price they pay for holding the lives of others in their grasp."

"That is not what we are speaking of, and you know it."

"Perhaps not." He rose from the table with the slow, deliberate motions of an old man. "I must pay my respects to the French legate."

"Could I come with you?"

He hesitated, then decided, "No."

"I don't need to go in. I won't speak. I just want—"

"You want to escape. You want to explore. Alas, I cannot help you." His gaze carried the brooding depths of a man whose wounds had been exposed. "Your ambassador would not hear of it. And my own superiors would wonder what I am doing, escorting an American civilian through a civil war."

"Turkey is not at war."

"Not yet, no. But your ambassador is correct. The place is a tinderbox. I can already smell the city burning."

"I don't smell anything."

"You have not known war. I hope you never do."

"How long must I remain here?"

"Until the senator is invited to meet with the caliph. Days, perhaps. Longer. Perhaps never."

"What?"

"The ambassador has been seeking an audience for three weeks."

She waited until he was out of hearing range to protest, "I did not travel six thousand miles to be trapped inside a gilded cage."

: CHAPTER 16 :

:

Muriel spent the afternoon in the library. The embassy was housed in a palace which had once belonged to an Ottoman prince. A century earlier, the sultan had given it to the American government after they had assisted Turkey in a dispute with Russia. The embassy library was housed in what had formerly been the harem, a series of seven adjoining rooms. The largest chamber was adjacent to the main audience hall. The other six formed an *L* that extended over the stable block. The former baths had been turned into a reading room. The walls and ceiling were adorned with hand-painted ceramic tiles. Muriel read the documents related to the embassy's foundation and wondered about the women who had once dwelled here.

She divided her research into two components. First, she read what she could find about the current situation in Turkey. When she approached the librarian and requested certain documents, he frowned over his half-moon spectacles and refused point-blank. Muriel politely offered to find the senator and ask his help in locating the requested papers. The librarian departed in a snit, only to return and give her everything she requested.

The second portion of her research was about the reliquary itself. The embassy library was a treasure trove containing tens of thousands of books, pamphlets, official documents, maps, and globes. The largest of the bedchambers, the one that had belonged to the prince's senior wife, was given over to a private collection that had been deeded to the embassy by an American businessman who had lived and died in Constantinople. A plaque by the door dedicated the room to his memory. The shelves contained a wealth of information about the entire region.

She had often studied in such a fashion, splitting her time between two seemingly disconnected themes. Often, she found the topics fed upon each other, such that she would be deeply involved in one and suddenly find herself struck by an idea about the other. Which was precisely what happened that afternoon.

There were no clocks, and all but one of the harem's windows were narrow slits set high up in the walls. The only exception was a balcony set over the street and surrounded by beautifully carved wooden latticework. The balcony was intended to grant the women a chance to see the outside world while keeping them from being observed by passersby. The narrow balcony was stiflingly hot and shrouded in shadows even while the street below blazed with afternoon sun. Muriel worked at a long central table that she had gradually filled with her two areas of research. Which, because of her idea, had melded into one unified concept that left her so excited she felt she might burst.

Even so, she did not speak of it when Senator Bryan arrived. She lifted a pile of nineteenth-century pamphlets off the chair at the head of the table. The senator surveyed the table and did not notice as she dusted the padded leather seat with her sleeve. "You certainly have been busy. Has it been fruitful?"

"I think so, yes."

"Then at least one of us has found some benefit to the day."
He dropped onto the chair with an exasperated sigh. "All of
the embassies have been ordered to remain cloistered away. By
order of the caliph himself. For their own safety. This afternoon
word arrived that the sultan may in fact order the closure of all
Western embassies. How on earth we are supposed to go about
our business while imprisoned within these walls is beyond me."

Muriel glanced around the chamber, thinking of the generations of women who had moved in here and never left. Some,
she knew from her research, had been as young as thirteen.
Others, girls born into the harem, had been gifted as wives to
men they had never met, trading one elegant prison for another.

"Our contact is Sultan Ahmet, principal advisor to the caliph.
I have sent word to him by way of a messenger, a Turk who
works here and no doubt spies for his own government. They
are the only ones allowed beyond the embassy gates. The French
legate is the only one in Constantinople permitted to travel
about freely. The ambassador tells me the prince's hands are tied
as well. The caliph has ordered his own cabinet to be sequestered, just like us. He does not trust them, you see. He fears they
might turn against him and pledge loyalty to the opposition."
He drummed his fingers on the tabletop. "The rivals are led by a
man named Atatürk, an upstart general from the hinterlands."

"I have been reading up on him."

"Have you indeed." But her words did not seem to register
with the senator. "I am not good at waiting. I feel stifled, as
though my air is being cut off. Why on earth aren't there any
windows to this place?"

"It is the harem."

"Eh, what's that?"

Muriel did not want to share her idea with him when he was in such a state. "Would you care to see something special?"

"Oh, very well. I suppose…" He did not want to come, and he did not want to stay. But he followed her through the interconnecting rooms. The librarian glowered at them as they passed, but Senator Bryan did not appear to notice the man at all. "We have come so far and have gotten so close, but now, I fear…I dare not even say what I fear."

She led him through a pair of carved wooden doors and out into a walled garden. Rose bushes climbed the high stone walls. The shadows were thick here, and a faint trace of wind found its way down into the space, bringing a hint of coolness. Muriel pointed them to stone benches set by a central fountain. "We can sit here."

The senator settled on the bench, fiddled with his watch chain, squinted at the patch of blue sky overhead. Gradually he relaxed enough to take in his surroundings. "What on earth is this place?"

"The harem gardens. The walls are intended to shield the women from view, even from the highest windows."

The fountain was framed by a shimmering pool fashioned from the same painted tiles as the women's bath. As they sat, a pair of birds flew in to drink. They were small as robins but with breasts of brilliant gold. Muriel watched them flutter away and felt bonded to the women whose only hint of freedom had come from watching birds go where they could not. Year after year.

When she turned back, she saw that the senator had managed to set aside his worries enough to hear what she had to say. Muriel announced, "I think I may have found us a way forward."

• • •

That night she dreamed again of standing at the foot of the cross. It only lasted a second or two, and perhaps that was why she woke up without feeling the same sense of overwhelming sorrow. When she gasped awake, she felt a lingering aftereffect, like a fever now gone. Muriel rose from her bed and walked to the window. Four stories below her, in the embassy's main forecourt, a trio of Marines talked softly while another walked the periphery. Beyond the gates were more of the Turkish soldiers. The faint light reflected off their gold fez caps and their trousers' white stripes. They slouched and ignored the American soldiers inside.

Then the soldiers tensed, both those inside and those outside the main gates. The Turkish soldiers snarled at the Americans when they gathered by the entry, but there was no real force to the words, and the Marines ignored them.

Then Muriel heard it. The sound was very faint at first, a nervous rush of sound coming from several different locations. It intensified five or six streets away and seemed to move toward them, carried on so many footsteps they sounded like rain.

The mob yelled and shouted and then gathered together and stomped out a verbal cadence, one voice calling and then a thousand in response. Ten thousand. The sound was so great it echoed off the distant hills.

Suddenly the night erupted with a gold flash, then a massive *boom* resonated through her body. She did not hear it so much as feel it like an earthquake. The wind buffeted her with a fierce and careless fist. Four blocks removed from the blast, Muriel was almost knocked from her feet. The silence that followed was more dreadful than the explosion.

A woman's shrill scream sliced the night like a rapier. Dogs barked. Then gunfire erupted. A few shots, another scream, then a barrage so vicious she saw the light as one burning ember.

Then the night became hushed once more. Even the dogs went quiet. Muriel had never thought silence could carry such dreaded menace.

She slept no more that night.

: CHAPTER 17 :

:

When Muriel entered the dining hall that morning, there was a noticeable difference to the atmosphere. The waiters politely offered her an Oriental breakfast of cheese and dates and hot flatbread and spiced tea. But their eyes were clouded, their smiles forced. Charles did not appear. The soft conversations at other tables carried a worried, fretful tone.

Then the senator appeared with the ambassador. There was a second room, smaller than the main hall, where the senior diplomats took their meals. Senator Bryan crossed the room, wished her a good morning, stared at her plate, and asked, "What on earth is that?"

"What the locals eat. Charles arranged it. We both found the standard fare...difficult to digest."

The ambassador sniffed, "My wife has spent two years trying to teach them how to cook properly. They cannot even percolate a proper cup of coffee."

Senator Bryan did not smile. His face showed no real reaction at all. But Muriel had the impression that he was very pleased. "Ambassador, be so good as to instruct your kitchen that from now on I will have what the lady is having. Muriel, I would be grateful if you would join us in the other room."

The room was paneled in mahogany that was carved to resemble vines climbing a trellis. One panel up by the ceiling had become so water stained and warped it peeled away from the wall. The two windows were stained glass, such that the room was bathed in odd combinations of orange and red. Muriel refused the waiter's offer of more food and sat watching the others.

The ambassador's narrow features creased with displeasure. He fretted over his plate, then pushed it aside with an irritated gesture. Joining them was the ambassador's chargé. Edward Vaughan was a small man with an oversized belly that seemed barely contained by his glittering vest. He wore sideburns so long they almost joined with his moustache. The librarian sat at the oval table's far end and glared at her over a cold cup of coffee.

"I am interested," the senator said, "in learning what you found in your research that led you to make yesterday's suggestion."

"I told you it was a mistake to allow her access to embassy documents," the librarian protested.

"The senator insisted," the ambassador said sourly.

"Indeed so." The senator's expression carried a certain gleam, a barely repressed energy that neither the diplomats' sour mood nor the previous night's events could extinguish.

Muriel sat alone and isolated, the gleaming inlaid table a barrier between her and these men of jealous power. Muriel took a long breath and then began, "We face two problems. Or so it appears to me. First, there is the caliph's recent decree isolating the embassies. Second is the fact that the caliph actually holds no power whatsoever."

"Really, this is absurd," the ambassador said. "If you will excuse me, Senator, I have work to do."

"You are *not* excused. This not only pertains to your work, it *defines* your work. We will hear the lady out. Continue, if you please."

Muriel ignored the ambassador's glare as best she could. "The caliph is not in fact a caliph at all. The caliphate of Medina and Mecca was an honorary title assigned to the Ottoman sultan. But the Ottoman Empire ceased to exist at the end of the Great War. Allied forces conquered Baghdad, Damascus, and Jerusalem during the conflict. Two years ago, they divided the Ottoman Empire among themselves at the San Remo conference. France took a mandate over Syria, the British took control of Palestine and Mesopotamia, and the Turks were left with a fraction of their land. This fueled the uprising led by Mustafa Kemal Atatürk, which has set up a so-called democratic government in Ankara. The last sultan, Mehmed the Sixth, was deposed eight months ago and sent into exile. And this has left the United States and the European allies in a quandary."

Senator Bryan was openly smiling now. To Muriel's surprise, his expression was mirrored by the chargé, who had slid his chair back far enough to mask his expression from the ambassador. The senator asked, "Why are we troubled by this?"

Muriel continued, "Three reasons. First, the election was far from democratic. No opposition candidates were allowed to stand. Atatürk won by mandate. Second, no Western government has recognized Atatürk or his government. Which leads to the third issue."

To their surprise, the chargé said, "The present caliph."

The ambassador protested, "Really, Edward. Must you—"

"Go on," the senator insisted.

"Sultan Abdülmecid is a ruler in name only. He was appointed caliph after his cousin, Mehmed, was sent into exile. He is here so that the Europeans and the Americans can't say that the legitimate Ottoman ruler has been overthrown. The edicts you worry about don't come from the Abdülmecid at all. They are Atatürk's way of reminding you that real power now lies in Ankara, and it is time the Western governments recognize it."

The chargé said, "You read my report."

"Twice," Muriel said. "It was excellent."

The ambassador snorted. "Really, Senator, if it were only half as simple as Miss Ross makes it out to be, we wouldn't be in this predicament at all. And Edward's report has been repudiated by any number of experts in Washington. The uprising continues, as we all witnessed last night. The caliph is the ruler of Turkey. The rest is supposition and poppycock."

The senator leaned back so as to share a grim smile with the chargé, then said to Muriel, "Tell me about the caliph."

"Abdülmecid was chosen to rule because he has no interest whatsoever in politics or power. He is also named General of the Ottoman Army but has never served a day in the military, and the Ottoman Army itself no longer exists. He devotes his days to his two passions, collecting butterflies and painting."

This caught everyone by surprise, even the librarian, who exclaimed, "Where on earth did you come up with that?"

"A pamphlet in your library," Muriel retorted, "written by the Italian legate."

"You read Italian, I suppose?"

"He wrote in French," Muriel replied. "The language of diplomacy."

Senator Bryan coughed discreetly. "Which leads you to your idea."

"The caliph's favorite paintings are those he has made of his harem," Muriel confirmed. "I just wondered if he might like to have photographs taken. This work must be done by a woman, since no man other than the caliph is permitted entry."

"Which is why," the senator told the ambassador, "I sent her pictures to the caliph, along with a suggestion that I be allowed to accompany her."

Muriel looked from one face to the next, the sulking librarian, the fuming ambassador, the gratified senator, the grimly smiling chargé. She saw what she had missed before, the underlying frisson, an electric charge to the atmosphere, like before a summer storm.

"Why is this important?"

"We have received word that the caliph will reply this afternoon."

"He hasn't said yes," the ambassador muttered.

The senator exchanged another tightly wound smile with the chargé. "When was the last time the caliph responded to any of your queries, sir?"

The muscles in the ambassador's jaw bunched and writhed. He stared at his hands and did not speak.

• • •

The caliph's personal guards were known locally as Seljuks, after the dynasty that ruled Turkey a thousand years earlier. The ten who came from the palace were huge and silent and stood over six feet tall. They wore peaked caps instead of helmets, which added another ten inches to their height. Their uniforms were a fanciful combination of Western military and Oriental garb. Their trousers bore bright crimson strips down both legs, which they tucked into glossy black boots with silver chains at the top. More silver dangled from their right shoulders and from the broad belts holding both scimitars and pistols. Their moustaches were waxed and curled and woven into their sideburns. Their eyes blazed with centuries of fierce contempt.

They arrived in the early afternoon with Muriel's official summons. A private messenger had arrived earlier to warn them that the caliph was indeed going to respond and that they must be prepared to depart at a moment's notice. The caliph's invitation was a royal command and was to be obeyed without an instant's hesitation.

Muriel was joined in the ambassador's Daimler by Senator Bryan, the ambassador, his chargé, and Edward's wife, who proved to be fluent in Turkish. Muriel had insisted upon being accompanied by a woman who spoke the language. Sarah Vaughan shared her husband's brightly intelligent gaze and had mobile features that seemed constantly ready to break out in a smile. When the three men started talking softly among themselves, she whispered to Muriel, "I couldn't believe it when Edward asked if I wanted to serve as your companion. I haven't been out of the compound for weeks. I'm not even allowed to go to the market. I was ready to scream. And I would have, if I had thought it would do any good."

"Where did you learn Turkish?"

"I studied with a local tutor. Languages have always come easily for me."

"I wish I could say the same. I speak only French, and it took years of sweating over the books."

"Turkish is a fascinating tongue. There are elements of Arabic and Hebrew and ancient Mongol dialects, all rolled into a language that contains a thousand different ways to hide the truth in plain sight."

Muriel turned back to the window and the city. But she found it impossible to enjoy the journey. Her mind swirled with all she had learned about the current state of affairs. The city's din was punctuated by her memory of the explosion and gunfire from the previous night.

For six hundred years, the Ottoman Empire ruled the Caucasus, the Middle East, Greece, parts of Central Europe, and much of North Africa. But it began to crumble almost as soon as it was built. The sultans feared technology and despised the bustling frenetic energy of the Industrial Revolution. Russia was continually invading from the north, seeking to ignite a war that would allow it to swallow the Ottomans whole. The regime also suffered from rampant corruption. When the Allies invaded Turkey during the Great War, the whole house of cards came tumbling down.

France and Britain and America left a few troops in Turkey, propping up the caliph whom they intended to treat as a puppet. But the rise of Atatürk and his generals changed all that. Atatürk did not attack directly. Instead, small uprisings erupted in one place after another, with no direct tie to the hands that controlled them, much as the Allies were doing through the shadow caliph. The Allies could have brought in more troops and stamped the upstarts into the dust, of course. But the West had lost all appetite for further war. So the Allies watched helplessly as Atatürk won gradual control of Turkey. Eight months earlier, the newly elected Turkish parliament ordered the caliph to leave the country. Despite the Allies' plea for him to stay, Mehmed packed up and departed for a villa on the Italian Riviera. In his place, the parliament appointed Mehmed's cousin, Abdülmecid. Who ruled over nothing, and according to the documents Muriel had read, cared little either way.

They passed three large gatherings along the way. According to Sarah, two were in support of Atatürk, the third in favor of the caliph. This third group cheered wildly when the Seljuk guards came into view, trotting on horses as massive as the soldiers themselves. Six of the guards bore tall spears from which fluttered flags adorned with Arabic script. When the other two crowds spotted the Seljuks, they roared their defiance and started to rush forward. But the lead guards aimed their deadly spears straight at the people, while the others drew their guns. The crowd halted. The lead soldiers then flicked their reins, and the procession continued on.

The Daimler was a massive beast of a car with a wicker compartment for the passengers and a separate open seat for the driver and his companion. Charles Fouchet sat beside the driver in the forward compartment. Earlier that day, the senator had sent word to the French legate of their journey. When the ambassador protested, Senator Bryan replied that the French would most certainly hear of it, and probably already had. This way, they might defuse a problem before it arose. Now the ambassador fumed but said nothing, no doubt for fear that the senator would visit the caliph without him.

The procession traveled through streets that revealed a gray and crumbling city. Occasionally, Muriel glimpsed fragments of former grandeur—a wall made from painted tiles, a gilded balcony, a palace rising behind guarded gates. But the scars of war and neglect were everywhere. Especially on the faces of the people they passed.

Charles had not spoken with her when he arrived from the French embassy. His only acknowledgment had been a solemn nod in her direction. Then he had gone inside to confer with the ambassador. He sat ramrod straight in the open front compartment. Muriel stared at his back and wondered if she had made a mistake in suggesting that he be included.

They turned onto a broad avenue that flanked the Bosphorus Sea. A wall then rose up between them and the waters, so tall it cast the entire street in shadows. Along its length, every twenty meters, a pair of guards stood at rigid attention. The wall was unadorned save for occasional guard towers and continued for well over a mile. Finally, they arrived at a wide turning and the royal gates. Two massive guardhouses were connected by a galleried arch. Flags fluttered in the hot wind. The wall continued on down the lane until it melted with the dusty haze.

Their procession was saluted through the gates. They entered a different world. The fragrances of countless flowers filtered through her open window. Peacocks cried from the emerald lawns, and overhead she caught the flash of tropical birds in flight. The gardens were immaculate and stretched into the distance. The senator said, "I have heard the caliph's private gardens are larger than all of Alexandria."

The palace itself was so vast it was hard to take it in. Her research had included numerous descriptions penned by astonished diplomats. The main structure alone covered half a million square feet, a carved stone jewel set in an emerald field.

As Senator Bryan rose from the Daimler, the gilded portals opened, and guards flanking the doorway snapped to attention.

Muriel and Sarah took the camera equipment from the Daimler's massive trunk and followed the men up the stairs. The waiting majordomo was dressed in a cutaway jacket and striped formal trousers. He bowed a welcome and asked, "Which is the American photographer, please?"

"I am."

"Your name, please, it is what?"

"Ross. Muriel Ross."

"This way, if you please, Madame."

"I would like to bring my companion."

"A woman, yes? But of course. The both of you may come this way."

The ambassador protested, "We were expecting to see the caliph."

"And you are?"

"The United States ambassador, and this is Senator Bryan, who has traveled six thousand miles for this audience."

"Yes, yes, we received this note also. Very well, you also may enter."

"But will we see the caliph?"

"Perhaps. Yes, perhaps. I will certainly present Sultan Abdülmecid with your names." He ushered them inside. "Please."

As they stepped into the entrance gallery, Muriel stepped up close to Charles and asked, "Are you all right?"

"My ambassador is furious."

"With you? Why?"

"He feels he should be here instead of me. I refused. The senator's invitation was specific. The man is petty and vengeful. He intends to crush my career."

"Perhaps you should not have..." But the procession moved forward, and Muriel left the sentence unfinished.

The *Dolmabahçe* Palace took thirteen years to build and was completed in 1856. Muriel had doubted much of what she had read in the embassy library. But as they entered the first formal gallery, known as the Crystal Staircase, she decided that the descriptions had in fact not done the place justice.

The double arms of the stairwell were floored in marble, but the banisters and pillars were fashioned from crystal. The banisters were thicker than her leg, and there were hundreds of supporting columns. The crystal staircase was the largest article ever to come from the Baccarat factories in France. Muriel and the others climbed the carpeted steps and gaped at the central chandelier, a gift from Queen Victoria that weighed over five tons.

At the top of the stairs, the majordomo halted and pointed Muriel to his left. "You will please to enter the Harem-i-Humayun through those doors there."

Muriel hesitated, then asked, "Before I go, could I please see the Muayede Salonu?"

The majordomo smiled, revealing two gold molars. "You are speaking Turkish?"

"I read the name in a document yesterday. Please excuse my pronunciation."

"No, no, is very good." He stowed his smile away and bowed her forward. "This way, if you please."

The Muayede had been the point at which words had failed every observer. As soon as the Ceremonial Hall's enormous doors were drawn open, Muriel understood why.

The palace had cost over a million ounces of gold to build. The ceilings and walls of the Ceremonial Hall were gilded with over a ton of gold leaf. The floors were an intricate mosaic of semi-precious stones set in Carrara marble. Pillars of rose quartz extended down both sides of the six-hundred-foot-long chamber. Far, far in the distance, upon a dais of gold and onyx, stood the empty throne.

The majordomo gave them a moment, then said, "The gentlemen are to come and wait in the Medhal. Mesdames, if you will now proceed to the harem, the ladies await you."

: CHAPTER 18 :

:

The palace women were quiet and reserved and reluctant to meet Muriel's gaze. The children were like children everywhere, shy and excited in turn. The rooms were ornately decorated and stuffy. The women refused to respond when Sarah asked their names.

Muriel had no idea who they were, maid or wife or concubine, except through the ornate nature of their dress. There were many, many women, aged from infants to the seventies. The only boys were young children and a pair of eunuch guards who followed Muriel everywhere she went.

Since the women refused to utter a word, Sarah talked with the children. They scampered about, sheepishly answering her. The youngest hid behind the women's robes. Muriel used the Graflex for several group portraits, the women stiff and severe, the children somber. Then she stowed away the large camera and walked slowly through the six formal chambers, using the light and shadow to photograph the occupants. She shot four rolls of film and spent over two hours on her knees, sitting quietly, waiting and watching and absorbing.

Tea was served by maids as brightly dressed as their mistresses. Muriel and Sarah remained isolated throughout. But as she drank, Muriel sensed a presence and looked up to find a middle-aged woman watching her closely. She gestured with her cup in the direction of the French doors leading to the gardens. Muriel hesitated, then nodded once in response.

The woman set down her cup and rose to her feet. She stepped up to the eunuch, touched his arm, and spoke a few soft words. The man's upper arms were almost as thick as Muriel's waist. He wore a sash of woven gold about his vast middle and golden bands around his wrists. He pursed his lips, then nodded once. The woman glanced again in Muriel's direction and left the room.

Muriel rose and said to Sarah, "Wait here."

"But shouldn't I come..."

"Stay. Please." Muriel followed the stranger from the room, feeling eyes tracking her every step.

The enclosed garden was filled with brilliant sunlight and was so vast it was almost possible to ignore the high stone walls. Six fountains sprayed perfumed water and cooled the air. A bird with long, golden plumage stood so still Muriel thought at first it was a statue. Then it cocked its head so as to watch Muriel pass.

The woman continued through the garden, pausing only once when a child's voice called plaintively from the room they had left. She turned back and responded in a voice that almost sang with her calm assurance. Muriel was left with the comfortable sense that this woman meant her no harm.

Muriel followed her down a path that was almost lost to the vines and the flowering shrubs. At its end was an ancient door, so small and narrow it appeared made for children. But there was nothing childish about the warning look that the woman gave Muriel. "Do not speak. Do not even breathe loudly."

"How do you come to speak English?"

The woman's gaze carried centuries of secrets. "Hush now. All questions must wait."

She drew an elaborately carved key from the folds of her gown and slipped it into the lock. The door opened silently, and the woman stepped inside. Muriel had to lower herself almost to her knees to fit through the portal.

Inside was a web of shadow and light. The hall was so narrow her arms grazed the two walls, one of stone and the other of carved latticework. The woman moved silent as the shadows and stopped where the light did not enter. She turned and gripped Muriel's arms, her fingers carrying a dread warning. Carefully she moved Muriel forward, an inch at a time.

When she saw the scene that was revealed, Muriel started to gasp, but the woman's grip tightened in admonition.

The lattice was carved from sheets of marble. The stranger's hands kept her from approaching too closely, so that Muriel remained encased by shadows. It also permitted her to see through the lattice, like she was looking through a stone net. On the other side was the Medhal, the caliph's waiting room. Charles stood by the narrow windows, frowning into the afternoon light. The ambassador angrily paced the circular chamber. The senator and the ambassador's chargé sat on a padded onyx bench and talked softly.

The stranger allowed Muriel to study the scene for a moment, then drew her back down the hall and out into the sunlight. Muriel watched her lock the door, then followed her down the secret path. When they were again by the perfumed fountain, she asked, "Who are you?"

"My name is Shayla. I am wife to the grand vizier. I am also friend to the caliph's senior wife. She invited me to join you this day."

"Where did you learn your English?"

"My husband served as a diplomat in Washington under the former caliph, Mehmed. Unlike most Ottoman officials, my husband chose to take his family with him." She motioned Muriel toward one of the stone benches lining the fountain. "Deniz knew the end was near. He wanted me and the children to see America. He wanted us to understand we had a decision to make. Not then, not even that year. But soon. And now the time has come."

"Why are you telling me this?"

"The caliph will not see your ambassador. The caliph sees no one. He has received instructions from Atatürk to refuse all audiences. This suits him. He despises everything to do with power. He is only too happy to pretend to hold office. Atatürk has promised him a life of ease in Paris when this is done." Shayla stopped and waited.

Muriel read the silence and offered, "Atatürk is making no such promises to you and your husband."

"Deniz fears that once the revolution is complete, the citizens will demand that someone be put on trial. My husband would make the ideal criminal. We are Christians, and for us life has become increasingly difficult. Plus, my husband's family has served the sultans for eleven generations, mine for six. Our children…" She gathered herself. "You seek the reliquary, yes?"

"That is why we are here."

"Your senator claims that you are an expert in these matters. Is this true?"

"Reliquaries have been my field of study for several years."

"My husband will give it to you. In exchange, we want American citizenship. For the five of us. My husband, myself, and our three children. And you must help us escape."

"I don't know how—"

"There is to be no bargaining. The terms are what they are. The reliquary for our freedom." She rose to her feet. "Tomorrow morning at ten, come to your embassy's main gate. A trusted messenger will arrive. He will speak English, and he will offer you greetings from Deniz. Give him your answer."

: CHAPTER 19 :

:

The entire journey back, the ambassador and the senator remained locked in argument. Senator Bryan saw how disturbed Muriel became by their talk and tried to smooth the troubled waters by describing it as a spirited diplomatic exchange. But for Muriel a quarrel was a quarrel.

By dinnertime, cables had been exchanged with the State Department. Edward Vaughan was busy preparing the required documents. But still the squabbling continued. Muriel refused to join them for dinner and instead sat with Charles in the main dining room.

"This is the price of getting anything done in the diplomatic world," Charles said.

She could hear the raised voices through the connecting doors. "How you can stand this is beyond me."

"There are worse ways to resolve a dispute. War, for example."

"It's as though the last conflict taught them nothing."

"They are not arguing over the vizier's demands."

"Oh, I know that." She disliked how the friction was affecting her own state, yet felt helpless to change things. "It's about turf. Isn't that the word you use?"

"That is the correct term, yes, but it goes far deeper. The ambassador has staked his reputation on following the line set down by his allies in Washington. They insist that the caliphate can be saved. That Atatürk will fail. My own superiors want the same thing, even though it would result in a continuation of the same conflict they have had with America and Britain for fifty years."

"But why?" She did not realize how loudly she had spoken until heads turned toward her around the hall. "What on earth could be the benefit of such a move?"

"It protects them from the unknown."

She found herself settled, not so much by his explanation as the manner in which Charles spoke. She saw once more the officer who had commanded men in battle, the ability to size up a situation under the heat of war.

"Out there are a thousand questions, for which neither Paris nor Washington have answers," Charles went on. "Atatürk represents a total loss of control. Yes, they have bickered for fifty years over Turkey and the Bosphorus. But there are rules that govern this dispute. With Atatürk, they are powerless to even guess what might happen. They sought to prop up the caliphate, but Atatürk has turned the West's attempts into a mockery. One that they are powerless to do anything about."

"The ambassador and his allies are afraid."

"As are many French officials," Charles agreed.

"Why don't they try to forge an alliance with Atatürk?"

"I suspect that is why the senator came."

"He came for the reliquary."

Charles nodded slowly. "So he has insisted all along."

"You don't believe him?"

Charles did not reply.

"Have you been infected by the same suspicions and mistrust as your minister?"

Charles remained silent.

She found herself saying, "Senator Bryan warned me about you."

"I would never harm—"

"He said you might have lost the desire to ever heal. Or allow yourself to know God's peace."

The stern visage turned dark, as though Charles had the ability to suck the shadows from the room and apply them to his features. "I admire the senator's ability to believe in anything these days."

"Then why not share his faith?"

"It is a question my wife would have liked, or perhaps even asked herself." His voice grated, raw and harsh. "Look where it took her. And our child."

Muriel leaned forward, drawn to him by a sense of desperate yearning, a desire she had denied she even felt until that moment. To love this man. To claim a future together. If only... "Charles, look at me. Please."

His dark gaze swiveled about, but she could not tell if he saw her at all. She said, "Pray with me."

He blinked slowly. Again.

"Please. For both our sakes. For the life that could be yours to—"

"Anything I said would be a lie." His voice carried the dismal quality of the night beyond the windows. "And I respect you too much for that."

She forced herself to rise from the table. She nodded once, then turned away. There was nothing more to be said.

• • •

That night Muriel dreamed of the cross again. As before, when she awoke she found herself gripping the simple wooden crucifix she wore around her neck, and her pillow was wet with tears. Yet this time she felt oddly at peace.

She rose and washed her face and went to stand by the window. The night was overcast, the clouds turned coppery by the lights rising from the city. On a distant hill, a building burned. She heard shouts and the occasional gunshot. Constantinople looked like a forge upon which blazed all the chaos and passions that mankind was capable of producing. Muriel shut her curtains and returned to sit upon her bed.

She knew why there was no sorrow. The dream had not returned to convict her. She knew she was a sinner. She knew her only hope of eternity lay in the Savior's gift. No, the dream had returned because she needed to focus. She was surrounded by the din and tumult of life and conflict and war. She had every reason to think on all the other things in her world besides this. The one essential element. Her reason for coming. Charles was wrong, she knew. The senator was a man who moved through the world and yet remained strong in his faith and his convictions. She could trust him. She could use him as an example.

As she lay back down, she reflected on what her father had said in their too-brief telephone conversation. She found herself wanting the same thing. To be known as a good and willing servant. To be faithful to her calling, and this quest. To do what was required, to the best of her ability.

She fell asleep to the sound of approaching gunfire. She slept and did not dream.

: CHAPTER 20 :

:

Muriel was almost finished with breakfast when Charles appeared in the dining room doorway. He did not so much look at her as take aim. He crossed the room, almost colliding with a man returning to his seat from the coffee cistern. Charles gave no sign he saw the man at all. He looked over her table. "I must speak with you."

"Of course." Charles looked as though he had not slept. His eyes were sunken, his cheeks cavernous. "Do you want to go elsewhere?"

"Here, another place, it does not matter. We are never alone. We are always..." He collapsed into the seat. "I must ask you something. You must tell me the truth."

"Of course I will. I always have."

"Yes, that is who you are, is it not? The teller of truths."

"Did you sleep at all last night?"

"Some. Badly. The dreams..." He wiped his face. "It would have been better if I had not slept at all."

"Do you want something to eat?"

"No food. Answers." He leaned forward. "How do you know Senator Bryan tells you the truth?"

"You mean, about our being here in Constantinople to find the reliquary?" Out of the corner of her eye, she noticed

Edward, the ambassador's chargé, watching them with concern. She raised one hand, motioning for him to keep away. "Will you tell me why this is important, Charles?"

"It is crucial. Is that not enough?"

"Yes, of course it is." Muriel addressed him as she would a feverish child, keeping her voice level, her tone mild. "Let me tell you what I know, and then you may make your own decision. Would you like that?"

"What *I* like," he muttered. "What difference does it make in this horrid world what I like or want?"

"It matters very much to me," she said.

"Then answer my question."

"Very well, Charles. First, I have known Senator Bryan all my life. He and my parents have been friends since before I was born. When I became fascinated with photography, he gained access for me to places in our nation's capital. His interest in me grew once I entered university and chose to study history. He urged me to take every course the school offered in Roman antiquities. Which I gladly did. I found myself captivated by the period known as early Byzantium, when Christianity became the religion of the Roman Empire. And I liked the attention of this powerful man."

Charles eased back in his chair. A number of the others watched them. He either chose to ignore their stares or did not see them at all. "I don't see what any of this has to do—"

"Wait, please. You asked me a question that is clearly very important to you. I am trying to answer you fully. After I graduated, Senator Bryan helped me obtain a position as a researcher at the Smithsonian. I was the youngest researcher they had ever taken on, one of only a handful of women."

"He was your advocate," Charles said, and for some reason the words left a bitter taste. "Just as the minister is for me."

"Exactly. But most of the other researchers who had such powerful backers did poor work. I struggled very hard to overcome this stain and prove..."

She stopped because Thomas Bryan and the ambassador pushed through the padded doors leading to the private dining hall. The senator spotted the two of them together and frowned. Muriel gave her head a tiny shake. His frown deepened, but he did not approach their table.

Charles pressed, "Yes, you were saying?"

"I was assigned responsibility over the Smithsonian's collection of reliquaries. I see that interests you. I learned that Senator Bryan had specifically requested this."

"Did he ever tell you why?"

"In a sense, though at the time I found his answer very unsatisfying. He said that he wanted me, his friend, to be ready in case prayers were indeed answered."

Charles rubbed his face with one hand. He did not speak.

"Do you see, Charles? Your suspicions are unfounded. How could such a man as this possibly be here for any reason other than the one he has given us?"

"He spent his time in Paris doing the American president's bidding."

"Of course he did. He is a United States senator. But the duties of his station did not occupy *all* his time. He also accompanied me to Saint Denis and then to Notre Dame. And why was this? Because he needs to be certain that the reliquary we are here to recover is real. How is that possible? No records have survived the centuries since the reliquaries were first made. So he took me to Notre Dame to view the reliquary that has the clearest lineage. Since the moment it arrived from Rome to today, it has remained a part of recorded history. Think on that. Sixteen hundred years, through war and strife—"

"Enough." He bolted to his feet. "I have heard enough…"

She gripped his hand. "Sit back down, Charles. Please. I have a question of my own."

He stared at her hand on his and did not move.

"This isn't about the reliquary, is it? Nor is it about trusting Senator Bryan."

"Of course it is."

"Not at the deepest level. It's about something more. Something vital."

"Let go of my hand."

"You want to know how a man who has held power through the Great War can still maintain his faith."

"He saw nothing. He knew—"

"He sent young men to die in battle. Just like you. From a safe distance, yes, but you see the weight he carries from this time. Don't you? And yet he is different from the men you know in Paris."

"Release me. I won't ask you again."

She did as he demanded. "You don't care about his motives. You care about his *faith*."

He might as well have been turned to stone. He did not speak. He did not appear to even breathe.

"You want to know whether his faith in God is real. You want to know whether you can trust him to speak from a heart that has held on to the most vital part of his existence. And I am here to tell you that the answer to that question is yes, Charles.

I know because I share it. I know because I have prayed with him and seen the peace that fills him when he studies the Word. I know because…"

Wordlessly, Charles spun about and strode from the room.

When he was gone, Senator Bryan approached her and said, "Do you want to tell me what that was about?"

Now that it was over, she found herself aching from the fierce onslaught of emotions. "He is a man seeking answers only God can give."

The senator covered his unease by pulling the pocket watch from his vest and clicking it open. "We are due in the courtyard."

Muriel rose unsteadily from her chair. Her legs felt weak. As they passed through the dining room entrance, she said, "You were right all along. About Charles, I mean."

The look he gave her carried the sympathy of a lifelong friend. "The news gives me no pleasure whatsoever, believe you me."

• • •

The ambassador's driver was the lone occupant of the front courtyard. He washed and polished the embassy Daimler. He glanced up, hopeful that the ambassador would order to be taken somewhere. When they passed him without speaking, he returned to his work. The drive curved around the stone outbuildings that shielded the embassy's main portal from the street. Many of the diplomats' families were housed here. Muriel knew from overheard conversation that the children had been sent home to relatives, but even so, the accommodations were cramped and overcrowded, with as many as seven families sharing one kitchen. Muriel felt eyes on her as she approached the main gate.

The ambassador said, "I still feel it is a serious mistake to allow that man to observe the proceedings."

Muriel spotted Charles standing by the main entrance, watching them. He seemed barely separated from the portico's shadows.

"Your objections are duly noted," the senator replied.

But the ambassador was not done. "I'm convinced he is a spy."

"Of course he is." The senator held to a smooth calmness, similar to how Muriel had addressed Charles. "I *want* them to have an observer present."

The ambassador's mouth worked for a moment before he managed, "But...what on earth for?"

"For the same reason that you and Charles accompanied us yesterday," the senator replied. "So that the world will know there is no hidden motive, no grab for power, no possible conflict." He asked Muriel, "Ready?"

Together they walked the graveled drive. When the ambassador held back, Senator Bryan said, "You too, if you please."

Muriel protested, "They may not approach me if I'm not alone."

"I am well aware of that." The senator held to the same reasonable tone. "I merely want the watchers to see that you speak with our approval."

One of the Marines on duty stepped from the pillbox's shade. "Can I help you, Sirs?"

"Indeed you can, Sergeant." The senator pointed at the shrubs in the central island. "I'd like you and your associate to go stand over there."

"But sir..."

"Do as he says," the ambassador ordered.

"And leave your rifles in the guard box," Senator Bryan added.

Reluctantly, the two Marines set their weapons by the duty stations, then backed away. As they departed, Senator Bryan asked, "Have either of you gentlemen noticed anything out of the ordinary this morning?"

One of them muttered, "Other than a man who ain't in our chain of command ordering us to surrender our post?"

The other responded, "Them two Turks, the guards, they scarpered off, sir."

"When did that happen?"

"Few minutes before you arrived. First time I've ever seen them leave their posts."

"Thank you, gentlemen. All right, Muriel. It's most certainly time."

Together the three of them approached the tall metal gates. Outside the barred entrance flowed the chaotic street traffic of central Constantinople—overladen donkeys and camels, an occasional motor vehicle emitting clouds of exhaust, and people. A countless stream of people, walking and calling and shouting and gesticulating, in all manner of dress. Most of the women's faces were covered, but not all. They stood there for a few minutes, the ambassador fidgeting, the senator calmly observing, and Muriel. Finally, Senator Bryan said, "Come, Ambassador."

The ambassador protested, "But we don't know if they have spotted us."

"Oh, I think we can safely assume they have seen all they need to." Senator Bryan offered Muriel a confident smile. "Good luck, my dear."

She continued to watch the noisy tide. The only constant was how every face that passed stared at her. Dark eyes probed with cold hostility, then moved on. Until one man stepped away from the flow and approached. "You are the woman Miss Muriel Ross?"

"Yes. And you?"

"My name, it is not important."

"It is to me."

"Then I am Yussuf." His English was heavily accented but understandable.

"I have an interpreter ready, Mr. Yussuf."

"No one else." He wore the ragged clothes of a street beggar, and his face was streaked with dirt. But his features were clean shaven and intelligent. And young. He could not have been more than eighteen.

Muriel guessed, "You are the vizier's son?"

"Who I am is not the question. Do you have an answer?"

"We will do this."

"Citizenship for all the vizier's family. And safe transport to America."

"It is agreed." She gestured to the men standing by the central circle. "Their presence confirms it."

He examined her intently. "It is true, you are a researcher of the Christian church's ancient treasures?"

"I am. Your family is Christian?"

"If we were, then we would be wise to leave Turkey. Now take this." He slipped a tightly folded paper from his sleeve and passed it through the bars. "Tonight at midnight. Be ready."

And he was gone.

: CHAPTER 21 :

:

T he day was filled with planning. By lunchtime, the details had been laid out. The ambassador remained intensely displeased with the senator, who had insisted that Muriel be included in their discussions. Muriel listened carefully but offered nothing. In truth, she would have preferred to be upstairs in the library.

The ambassador dug in his heels when Senator Bryan requested they include Charles in the party. "Absolutely out of the question. I am astonished you would even suggest such a thing."

To her surprise, Senator Bryan turned to her and asked, "What do you think?"

"Really, Senator," the ambassador protested.

"Muriel Ross is a professional analyst," the senator replied. "What is more, her idea is the only reason we have made it so far. Our success depends upon her."

Muriel asked, "Will we have soldiers?"

The senator lifted the folded sheet of paper handed to her by Yussuf. "The vizier's instructions are clear enough. We may travel with three people only."

Muriel had studied the tightly scripted sheet with the others. Her question had been for the ambassador's sake. "Charles has known battle. If we are to face danger, he would be a worthy ally."

"My thoughts exactly."

"We have any number of highly capable veterans in our compound," the ambassador protested.

"None of whom have been with us since we arrived in Europe," the senator replied.

"You don't know the French like I do," the ambassador said. "They have crossed us at every turn."

"They helped us immensely while we were in Paris."

"But they are the only nation whose embassy is not imprisoned!"

"Which may actually harm them, once Atatürk completes his conquest of Turkey."

"You don't know that will happen!"

"Actually, I do," Senator Bryan replied. "And so do you."

The ambassador disliked that intensely. "If the French can halt us or impede our progress in any way, they will. You mark my words."

"Noted." Senator Bryan turned to Edward. "Be so good as to summon the gentleman."

When Charles entered, the senator handed him the sheet of paper. While he read, the ambassador paced impatiently. Finally, he handed back the page and said, "Thank you for trusting me, Sir."

"Your impression?"

"I will need a brace of pistols," he replied without hesitation. "And we will not be coming back."

• • •

The wind died after lunch, and the afternoon sun baked the compound. The street beyond the locked main gates was a noisy river of Turkish life. And yet within the embassy compound there was a sense of renewed purpose. Muriel observed how the embassy staff moved with greater intention. Cables were written and reviewed and sent. Charles brooded and spoke seldom, and when he did, the ambassador glowered. Muriel excused herself, saying she wanted to pack. In truth, all the talk had left her weary and unable to think clearly.

Packing required no time at all. She was restricted to one case. She was going to take her Graflex and the Leica, her two best outfits from home, and the three dresses from Chanel. As Muriel folded in the formal gown, she heard faint echoes of music. Above the dusty heat and the cries of donkeys and men drifted the faint refrain from a mythic opera house with red velvet walls and sparkling chandeliers. The music shifted, and Muriel recalled a quartet playing a Schubert concerto in the French president's palace. Then a choir sang a hymn over ten centuries old, as a priest who had defied the world's darkest hour lifted a fragment of the cross over his head. When she closed the satchel, Muriel felt as though she was saying farewell to a life that had never truly been hers to claim.

An idea struck her, and she carried the tripod and the Graflex back downstairs. She crossed the forecourt and entered the married quarters. She found Sarah and explained what she had in mind. Muriel then had to repeat herself three times, as more and more people crowded in around her. When the families excitedly agreed, Muriel moved back outside and studied the forecourt.

The afternoon sunlight fashioned irregular shadows from the palm and jacaranda trees. Muriel decided the best place for photographing the families would be on the first two embassy stairs. Further up would result in shadows from the portico's overhang.

Edward and Sarah arrived shy and hesitant as she was still setting up the tripod. She took her time, positioning Sarah on Edward's other side because she held their infant and Muriel wanted the sunlight full on the infant's face. The baby squinted, but there was nothing to be done about that. She took careful readings with the light meter, then slid a fresh plate into the camera. The Graflex's negatives were set on metal squares with thin sleeves to protect them from the light. Before releasing the shutter, the photographer slipped out the sleeve, took the picture, and then replaced the sleeve, pulled out the negative, turned it over, and shot the next picture. By this point, the actions came as naturally to Muriel as using the light meter. As she turned over the plate, a flock of gulls flew overhead. Muriel took the second photograph just as the infant raised her hands to try and catch the birds.

She was positioning the second family, the librarian and his wife and two children, when the ambassador emerged from the main building. He took in the mothers straightening their children's clothes and the happy chatter and the laughter, then glared at Muriel and stalked back inside.

Sarah stepped up beside her. "Don't mind him."

"Why is he so upset with me?"

"It's not you at all. It's what you and the senator represent." She swept her hand at the front gates. "Out there the world is changing. The ambassador has spent his entire life dealing with kings and emperors who no longer exist. He was certain the Ottomans would hold onto power. He's wrong. He knows he's wrong. And he is frightened."

"What will happen to him?"

Sarah smiled sadly. "In a few months, he will return to Washington and be swept aside. He will spend the remainder of his career in some windowless office, then retire, forgotten and unsung. You represent the future he will have no part of. My husband has already been appointed his successor."

"I suppose I should congratulate Edward for his promotion." She glanced out the barred entrance to the surging traffic and people. "But all I see out there is chaos."

"And you are right." Sarah continued to study the world beyond the barred gates. "But all beginnings are born in chaos, are they not?"

Muriel worked through the afternoon, shooting one family after another. Each time she was finished, the family handed her a paper with the address of those to whom the photographs would be sent. They smiled and spoke their thanks. For most, it was the first words they had uttered to her. Muriel did not mind. The ambassador was more than simply their boss. His disapproving presence defied the afternoon light. He dominated every aspect of their tiny enclosed world.

The shadows lengthened, and she finished the last of her plates. As she packed up her equipment, she decided this was a good way to seal her own time of change. Every negative she had brought with her had been used, forming slender records of her time in this alien world.

She climbed the stairs and resettled the folded dresses on top of the camera and the plates and forced the lid shut. She bathed and dressed in the same modest brown dress she had worn to the caliph's palace, then lay down on the bed and tried to rest. Her limbs ached from shifting the camera about and standing all afternoon and leaning down to peer through the viewfinder. Dinner was not for another hour, and the bed felt delicious. From beyond the window, a world of questions beckoned. Muriel had no idea what shape her future would take if she survived the night. But she sensed a great change in herself, a growing beyond the confines that had held her as tightly as the sleeves clenching the negative plates. She closed her eyes and again sensed the rising flow of distant music, a silent symphony just beyond the range of her hearing, beckoning her forward.

She woke to a knock upon the door. "Yes?"

Charles responded quietly, "It is time."

CHAPTER 22

Precisely at midnight, Muriel followed Senator Bryan and Charles through the embassy gates. The two Turkish guards gave no sign they saw anything at all. As Senator Bryan hefted his lone satchel, Edward clicked the gates shut behind him. The senator turned back and touched the chargé's hand through the metal bars. A single silent gesture of gratitude, then they were away.

A carriage waited on the avenue's other side. They made their way slowly through the nighttime flow of humanity and animals and commerce. Muriel's head still felt foggy from sleep, even though her heart was now racing. As they approached, the carriage door opened. They handed their luggage to the driver, who stowed them on the flat roof. Beside him sat a second man holding a shotgun. He gestured them to hurry with a jerk of his gun barrel.

When they stepped inside, they found the vizier's wife and three children huddled on one padded velvet seat. Shayla looked at Muriel and said in greeting, "The lives of my family are now in your hands."

The driver cracked his whip, and they set off.

The carriage was clearly designed to carry women. The window frames held ornately carved wooden friezes, and these were covered by a thin gauze. Muriel hated the effect. The world drifted by in blurred shadows and muted tones, punctuated by shouts and distant gunfire. They passed a burning building, and all she could see was what appeared to be specters dancing around its perimeter.

The night was steeped in palpable rage. Muriel could almost taste the anguish. The horses brayed nervously as the driver urged them on. Danger called to them from all sides. The youngest children huddled against their mother, and even the oldest boy, Yussuf, looked tense and scared. Charles fretted, "I should be up top with the driver."

"What would one gun do against the mob?" Senator Bryan replied calmly. "If they were to spy a foreigner, it may turn them against us."

The middle child whimpered. Senator Bryan turned to the little girl and smiled. "You speak English?"

"S-Some, Lord. A-A little."

"I am not a lord. And it sounds to me like you speak more than just a little. You lived in America, did you not?"

"My Miriam was born there," her mother replied.

"Miriam, what a lovely name. It suits you. Well, Miriam, we are doing our best to take you back there. To a home where you can live in safety."

Dark eyes watched him from the safety of her mother's arm. "No bangs?"

"No bangs, especially at night," he solemnly assured her. "Do you know, perhaps you might want to have a pet?"

Shayla stroked her daughter's forehead. "My Miriam wants a kitten more than anything in the world."

Only then did Muriel notice the excitement in Senator Bryan's eyes. She realized that the senator was enjoying himself. The danger was for him part of something greater, the sweep of events that shaped his world of politics and intrigue and power.

Muriel asked, "Where are we going?"

It was Yussuf who replied. "We are taking the southern route to Seraglio Point. We travel below the Grand Bazaar, where there is much fighting. Through the Sultanahmet Quarter, then along the Sea of Marmara."

The names were spiced by centuries of tales. Muriel yearned to cast aside the window veil and catch at least one glimpse of all that was so close. But when Charles touched the curtain over the frieze, Shayla said, "For the lives of my children, do not."

Charles did not look well. His eyes had sunk further into his skull. His skin was stretched tight over his features. There was a loud bang somewhere to their left, almost like a cannonade. Charles was the only one who did not flinch. He fingered the handle of his revolver and glared at all he could not see.

The journey was endless, or so it seemed to Muriel, but when they finally halted and the senator pulled out his pocket watch, she saw it was not yet two in the morning. Despite the continuous din, the two smaller children had fallen asleep, their heads cradled in Shayla's lap. The door opened, and a trim man who could only be Yussuf's father said, "Come, quickly, for your lives."

Wordlessly, Shayla handed the smallest child to her husband. She gathered up the middle girl and allowed her son and the senator to help her out. Swiftly, the driver passed down their belongings while the guard continued his tense observation of the night. The vizier led them through an entrance and into a shop selling Turkish carpets.

Senator Bryan muttered, "What on earth?"

"Quiet," the vizier hissed. "Follow me."

They passed through a narrow aisle formed by pillars of stacked carpets. The air was musty with the smell of wool and dyes. At the back of the store stood a terrified old man holding a pair of lanterns. The vizier took one, pressed several gold coins into the man's hand, and said, "Yussuf."

"Here, Father."

"Follow behind in last position. Carry the other lantern."

They passed through a portal that was scarcely larger than a crawl space and clambered down winding stone stairs. Centuries of use had shaped them into crescents, and the wet steps shone slick as oiled glass in the lantern light. Down and down they went, until Muriel's legs ached from the tension of keeping upright while balancing her heavy satchel. The walls glistened with mold and ancient grime. The air was close and dank.

At the base, she found herself in a cavernous space, big as a cave and lined with massive stone pillars. The vizier's lantern swung precariously as he helped his wife clamber onto a raised walk. His voice echoed through the cavernous space. "This way. Hurry."

As they started along the stone path, Muriel gasped.

Senator Bryan walked immediately behind her. "What's the matter?"

"I just realized where we are."

A hiss echoed back at them, but it only served to lower the senator's voice. "Tell me."

"The Basilica Cistern," Muriel whispered. "It was first built by Constantine himself, supposedly around a spring that has been lost to time. Above us is the floor to the first imperial palace and the church that served the royal family."

"So it's very old."

"It was reputed to be the first church Constantine founded, some twenty years before he publicly gave his life to Christ. Two hundred years later, the emperor Justinian tore down both buildings. The palace and the church had started to crumble. In their place, Justinian built what is now above us. The Hagia Sophia. The church of holy wisdom."

"And these caverns?"

The vizier swung his lantern high, pausing long enough to glare back at them. But he did not speak, which Muriel took as the only permission she was going to receive. "The cisterns were expanded around the year 500, when the Great Palace was built. At the time, it was the largest palace in the world, stretching over some two hundred acres. The great complex of buildings included royal apartments, state rooms, a hippodrome, and an audience chamber called the Hall of Gold."

They walked through a forest of stone pillars. At their feet was a dark lake that stretched out in every direction, further than the feeble light's reach. The only sounds were their labored breathing, the echo of their footsteps, and the soft drip-drip of water.

Senator Bryan murmured, "But why are we here?"

Muriel hesitated because they had reached what she suspected was their destination. The brick wall towered at the end of the path, at first glance like a barrier intended to mock the stone pathway's direction. But at its center was a lighter shade of stone, peaked like an oriental window and framed in granite.

The vizier murmured, "Please, Miss Muriel. Answer the senator if you can."

She whispered, "Because the cistern's eastern edge lines up

with the Daphne Palace and the Church of Saints Sergius and Bacchus."

A gold tooth gleamed from beneath the vizier's waxed moustache. "And why is this important?"

"Because beneath the two lay the caliph's treasure room."

"Most remarkable." The vizier addressed Senator Bryan for the first time. "I understand why you brought this lady."

He handed the lantern to Charles and slipped a key from around his neck. One segment of the stone slipped away to reveal a hidden keyhole. He turned the key with great effort, then said, "Together, please."

The door shuddered and creaked and finally slipped open far enough for them all to enter. They found themselves in a crypt, filled not with gold but with bones. The vizier and his son shut the door and locked it into place, and then the vizier allowed himself his first easy breath. "We can talk now."

The senator asked, "Are we safe?"

"Not until we have left Turkish soil, I am sorry to say." He led them down the central path, broad as an avenue and lined by hundreds of curved alcoves that stretched from floor to ceiling. All of them holding bones. "As the right hand of the caliph, I am keeper of all records. Last year I came upon a ledger which had been lost since the beginning of the Ottomans' reign. Which is less of a surprise than one might suspect. The entire cistern was only discovered eighty years ago. Before, it was merely a legend."

The vizier led them up a series of stone stairs to what must have been the nave of a private chapel. The curved front was decorated with remnants of a Byzantine mosaic displaying Christ with his right hand raised in benediction.

But Muriel had only a moment to observe the mosaic, for the vizier raised his lantern, and there on the dais was displayed a wonder and a dreadful mystery. Standing upon the carved stone chest was not *a* reliquary.

There were seven.

: CHAPTER 23 :

:

The sight was staggering. Seven burnished and intricately detailed treasures glowed in the lantern light. Perched upon the ancient stone surface, framed by the crypts and the shadows, they gave off the aura of ancient legends brought to life.

Thomas Bryan was the first to speak. "Which one is it?"

"That, my dear senator, is precisely the answer your researcher must provide."

"I don't understand. Why not take them all?"

"Because we can't."

"Why not?"

"I have given my word. More than that I cannot say." The vizier motioned Muriel forward. "Choose wisely, dear lady. The lives of my family depend upon it."

"This is preposterous," Senator Bryan sputtered. "You can hardly expect—"

"She will do this because she must. We will take with us the one true reliquary. Nothing else. That is the vow I was required to make." As the vizier turned to Muriel, the perspiration on his forehead shone in the lantern's light. "Begin."

Muriel asked, "How long do I have?"

"Until the hour before dawn."

She took a long breath, then climbed the stairs and approached the stone table.

The history of the Constantinople reliquary was shrouded in mystery. Too often, the historians Muriel had studied felt it necessary to describe every shred of the fables, even the ones they knew to be untrue. Muriel had taken a different approach to all the artifacts she analyzed. She had focused her research upon the few facts she could verify. Over time, this approach had become part of her reputation.

First, she sought to prove or disprove the writings and the claims and the supposed history. Only then would she turn to the artifact itself. To her astonishment, she was the first researcher to take this approach, studying the item only once she had cleared away the fog of speculation.

The facts which could be confirmed about the Constantinople reliquary were few, as was normally the case with any item that had survived seventeen centuries. Helena had left the major portion of the Cross in Jerusalem's Church of the Holy Sepulchre. When Jerusalem first fell to the Muslims in 614, the Sassanid emperor cut off a portion and took it with him to Constantinople. Thirteen years later, when Jerusalem was retaken, the conquering general demanded that the Muslim emperor return it. The emperor claimed it was lost, and over time, this segment vanished into the realm of myth and conjecture.

When the Ottomans began the battles to retake Judea, the Jerusalem church leaders decided it would be best to carve their remaining portion of the Cross into smaller segments. Some stories put the number at two, others four, and one authority claimed it was seven. In any case, only two of these survived.

The first and largest remained in Helena's church.

It was the second segment that concerned Muriel. This portion was carried by crusading knights into battle, held aloft by the knights dedicated to its protection. The Ottoman general Saladin defeated them at the Battle of Hattin in 1187, captured the reliquary, and took it back to Constantinople.

Three times Christian rulers attempted to ransom the fragment. Richard the Lionheart offered the caliph the equivalent of twice the annual income of his entire kingdom. All three requests were turned down. Over time, this fragment became known as the Constantinople reliquary.

When news of the defeat reached Jerusalem, the monks hid the remaining reliquary in the same cave where Jesus had been laid. There it remained for the centuries Judea spent under Muslim rule. Several church leaders, including the bishop of Jerusalem, were tortured and crucified in order to obtain this fragment. But the secret remained intact for over five hundred years.

The clearest description of the Constantinople reliquary came from the late medieval era, when an ambassador from France gained favor with the court and was granted the opportunity to view the reliquary. The ambassador confirmed the description fit with those from the year 800, when it had been copied as an icon painting. Unlike most reliquaries, this one was rectangular and formed from a solid block of silver. The block was inlaid in gold in the shape of a cross and then painted with enamel laced with crushed precious stones.

Muriel dismissed four of the reliquaries out of hand. They were copies from Spain and Malta. This left three, all of which she studied as carefully as she could beneath the light of two lanterns. The vizier and Thomas Bryan found a cluster of torches in one corner, but she ordered them put out when the flames created unwanted shadows and the smoke stung her eyes. She was aware of the others drifting about. She knew they spoke, and several times the youngest children cried aloud. But the sounds and the others' presence only touched her at the most superficial level. Her entire being remained focused upon the mystery, the quest. The reason for her having come here. The assignment for which she had trained all her life long.

An hour passed, then another. Finally, she decided one of the three could definitely be set aside as a later copy. Which left two. The problem was, both were true to the actual form, and yet quite different in detail. Which meant comparing one against the other yielded nothing. Both predated the medieval era, this much was certain. She guessed both had been fashioned before the year 500. The methods of crafting the metal and enameling the colors were true to the epoch. She could not find a lever or handle on either. Were she not certain of what she held, she would have suspected both to be solid silver.

She could feel the others growing increasingly impatient. It was not that she didn't care. She simply had no room just then for anything other than solving the riddle. Somewhere in the distance, there rose yet another discussion about taking all the reliquaries. The vizier's voice rose anxiously, piercing the veil of her concentration. "Do you think I would not have done this if it was possible?"

"Listen to what I am saying. We take all seven, we inspect them in calmer surrounds, we return—"

"Return *where*? Return to *whom*? The empire is collapsing! Revolution is in the air!"

"Precisely why we should take them all!"

"You can argue all you want. The conditions have been clear from the outset. We take the one true reliquary. One!"

"And if we cannot identify which is correct?"

"Do not even suggest such a thing!"

A third voice rose above the others, strident and feminine. "And I forbid any more of this conversation!"

"Shayla, please, we are—"

"You are disturbing the children! You are destroying the lady's concentration! You are clouding the air with your talk!" One of the children wailed in confirmation. The vizier's wife shushed the little one, then went on in a calmer tone, "No amount of discussion will change what we face. Muriel will identify the reliquary, we will depart, we will survive. There is nothing more to discuss. The quarreling is finished."

"But—"

"Finished, do you hear me? This discussion is over."

Muriel had not turned from the artifacts. When the cavern went silent, she forced the tension from her neck and shoulders, shifted the lantern closer to the two remaining reliquaries, and returned to her task.

She decided that she needed to forget the business of comparing one to the other. She needed to look at each as an individual item, and see if there was some way to confirm that it was not in fact a solid block of metal, that there was indeed hidden inside a fragment of the holy wood.

Then she saw it.

What she had needed was that separation, the drawing away from her inspection. Muriel had often experienced such moments, usually in prayer or church or waking in the middle of the night. She would have the impression of an idea being given to her, rather than coming from herself. This time, it was like a whisper formed from the lantern's hiss, a soft murmur below the level of thought or words.

The central figure in both was a portrait of Jesus, formed from the crushed stones and enamel mix known as ormolu. In one, he took the standard Byzantine form, two fingers from his right hand lifted in benediction. In the other, the hand was held open and outwards, so that the wound from the nails was revealed. What was more, the Savior's robe was opened to reveal the wound in his side. Muriel asked herself aloud, "Why didn't I see this before?"

There was the sound of approaching footsteps. "See what?"

It was highly unusual for paintings from this epoch to show the Savior's wounds. The paintings were intended as messengers of revelation, since the vast majority of people from that epoch could neither read nor write. Christ was depicted as the Risen Lord who offered grace and peace and wholeness to all who believed.

"What is it you see?"

Muriel did not respond. First, she turned the artifact over, revealing the silver backing. She then traced one finger across the Greek inscription written around the narrow sides, *By this ye shall know I am He.* There was a message here. A clue. If only...

"Muriel?"

She turned her attention back to the main face. As was normal, the central figure was encircled by the twelve disciples. She inspected each carefully. There were no keyholes, no indentations that might have suggested where one had been filled in.

One of the smaller portraits was loose, but given the reliquary's murky legacy, that was hardly a surprise.

Muriel became convinced this was the reliquary. The subtle differences were enough. She held in her hands the vessel. Inside was hidden a fragment of the Savior's moment of greatest tragedy, and humankind's greatest triumph.

All she had to do was prove it to the others.

Again she traced her fingers over the enameled figures surrounding Jesus. One in particular caught her eye, the portrait at the bottom right corner, the one that was slightly loose. She leaned in closer. She reached for the lantern without raising her face from the portrait. Someone drew it up and close for her, holding it so that her shadow did not block her view. She wanted to thank them, but just then she was too caught up…

She gasped aloud.

"Tell us what it is!"

She lifted her head. "He is frowning."

"What?"

She bent back over the artifact. The twelve figures were scarcely each an inch square. The detail was remarkable. The colors defied their age. And this small corner portrait showed something she had never seen before. The man scowled fiercely. This was an astonishment. The tradition was that all the disciples were shown as filled with the ecstasy offered to all believers.

She said, "It's Thomas."

"My dear, we don't…"

"Hold the reliquary. Tightly."

"Take the lantern." Thomas Bryan passed over the light. He moved around to the table's opposite edge and gripped the reliquary's sides. "All right. Now what?"

All she could think to say was, "Pray."

Muriel gripped the lower corner and placed her two thumbs upon the face of Thomas. She pressed down as hard as she could, fighting against the stubborn grip of centuries.

The image shifted slightly. And clicked.

She slid the image of Thomas up and over. A fraction of an inch at a time. Sliding it toward the wounds that Thomas insisted upon touching before he would believe.

As she moved it, a thin silver chain was revealed, connected to the image's underside.

She pulled it up to where the border touched the wound, and there was a second click. The wound itself rose up slightly, an oddly shaped fragment of ground rubies and enamel.

Muriel carefully slid the tiny portrait of Thomas back into place, then slowly placed her finger atop the Savior's wound. She too was a doubter. She too needed the concrete, the finite. Though it was a weakness, still she sought the miracle she could hold and claim as her own. She pressed down and heard a third click, one louder than the others.

The entire central portion popped up.

Muriel's hands were shaking so badly she had to stop and grip them tightly. The entire cavern seemed to be holding its breath. She pried open the facade, revealing a tight niche carved into the silver block, about three inches wide and ten long. Inside was cradled a block of wood, encased by the same silver frame she had last seen in Notre Dame.

A voice from deep inside the cavern's shadows declared, "Oh, I say, well done. Very well done indeed."

: CHAPTER 24 :

:

He had once been a very large man. Muriel could see that from the way his skin hung about his neck and jaw, slack folds from a time when he strode the world like a giant among men. Now all that was huge about him was his dignity.

His beard was long and silver white, his eyes pale and brilliant as a wash of sunlit water over pearls. The man's voice boomed even when speaking softly. "What is your name, child?"

"Muriel. Muriel Ross."

His face was a mirror into a different world. He was frail in the manner of the truly ancient, and yet life burned fiercely in his gaze. He wore the black robe of the Greek Orthodox, with a broad necklace of silver and gold links, each as large as Muriel's thumbnail, slung about his neck. The top of a gold crucifix peeked from his robe's chest pocket. His face bore so many seams and fissures it was impossible to guess his age. He walked stooped over, leaning upon the shoulder of a robed acolyte. At full height, he would have towered over Senator Bryan, who himself stood an inch over six feet. His feet shuffled slowly as he approached. He spoke English with a hodgepodge of accents. "When my friend agreed to my test, I never thought it would result in this. I am glad to be proven wrong. It is an answer to a

145

closely guarded prayer, one I have shared only with our God."
He inspected her closely, his gaze peeling away the layers.

"You are American?"

"Yes, Father. From Washington, D.C."

"Your nation's capital. Is it beautiful?"

"Some portions, Father. Very beautiful. Other sections are not
so."

"And this nation you represent, does it follow the Savior's
call?"

"Some portions, Father. Yes."

"And others?"

Muriel did not respond.

A smile emerged through the frost of his beard. "Yes, yes,
sometimes the only way to offer honesty is through silence.
Every good priest learns this early. Allow me to introduce
myself. I am Theodorus, bishop of the Church of Saints Sergius
and Bacchus. You have heard of this place, my child?"

"Yes, Father."

"Then share your knowledge with the others, and save me the
breath, will you?"

"The church was built in the year 527 by the emperor
Justinian upon the foundations of a chapel Constantine erected
for the sailors and fishermen of his new capital. When they
decided to build the new palace compound here, the seaman's
church moved further west to the Seraglio Point. The original
church became the center of worship in the palace compound
for the royal household. It is shaped in an irregular octagon of
columns on two floors, like circular balconies, that support a
broad central dome with sixteen vaults, one of the largest ever

constructed at the time. It is named after two Roman centurions who converted to Christianity in the decades after Christ's death. They were martyred." She hesitated.

"Complete your story, my child."

"The church was converted to a mosque in the early sixteenth century. It remains a part of the Islamic state to this day."

"Which means I am bishop to a church that no longer exists." The priest was smiling broadly now. "A fair representation of why we are here speaking at all."

He turned to the others and continued, "As little as thirty years ago, Greek and Cypriot Christians in this city numbered over half a million souls. They formed a city within the city and ran much of the commerce and the banking. Now they flee, all who can. But because they are not Muslim, they are required to have exit permits. Which have been almost impossible to find. Yet the office of one official, the man who stands before me now, has continued to help us in secret. Though the exodus pains me greatly, I can see that there is no future for them here, so they depart with my blessing, and our secret ally has earned my thanks and my trust. I do not claim the gift of piercing the veil of time. But I can read the winds. And I know that the era when Christians could live and work safely here is drawing to a close."

The vizier said softly, "You should come with us."

"My time on this great and troubled earth is also ending. Thank you, my friend. But I shall remain and preside over the remnant of my flock." He glanced lovingly at the wood encased in its silver frame. "And soon, with God's provision, I shall kneel at the wounded feet of my Savior and ask his forgiveness for all the half-deeds of a life only half lived."

Muriel stammered, "I don't understand. You are giving up the reliquary?"

"First of all, it is not mine to give. I have only been its care-taker for a breath of time. Second, the question was not whether it should stay, but rather, where should it go? And the answer has come from my own flock, those who have chosen to live in your homeland. They tell me of vast open spaces and great opportunities, of good people who worship the Risen One. And, of course, they speak also of the darkness and of a need for this great new land to be more firmly anchored in the faith." He pointed one quivering finger at the reliquary. "They say America would make a good home for this relic of our Savior's crowning glory."

Senator Bryan cleared his throat. "That has been my lifelong dream, sir. To bring a fragment and plant it in our land, where it may take root and grow a family of God."

The bishop's attention turned to the senator. "And you are?"

"Senator Thomas Bryan, at your service."

"So, a man who strides the halls of power and yet maintains his faith?"

"I try, Sir. As you said, I both yearn for the moment I shall meet our Savior and dread it."

"Do all those who serve your nation also serve our Lord?"

"Were it only so. Some do, but far from all."

"Still, it is a good thing, to find a new home in a place where there is a strong and vibrant faith. Very well. The test was made and the answer given. I am satisfied." He gave them the bene-diction, gazed longingly at the fragment, and then said, "May it serve your quest to lift up the faithful of your nation, and may you ever serve the one true King."

No one spoke as the bishop turned and shuffled away. Only when the door creaked shut behind him did Muriel take her first full breath in what seemed like hours.

: CHAPTER 25 :

:

The acolyte returned a few minutes later, took up one of the lanterns, and gestured for them to follow. When a child whimpered, the young man turned long enough to frown them into silence. He entered a narrow alcove between two rows of recessed crypts and pressed an unseen lever so that a segment of the wall slid back. Thomas Bryan and Charles lit torches, and together they entered a tunnel as old as Christendom.

Several times, Muriel heard a soft rushing against the left-hand wall and finally realized it was the noise of waves. She tried to fit together a map in her head as they moved on. The Hall of Gold had been the largest building in the palace complex, named after the formal audience hall at its center. Between it and the Sea of Marmara rose the Bucoleon Palace, once used to house the caliph's honored guests. There was then a sequence of buildings long thought to have once belonged to the caliph's senior officials, ending at the Church of Saints Sergius and Bacchus. She assumed they were following what once had been the fortress wall between the palace grounds and the Sea of Marmara. The tunnel could originally have been used for servants, soldiers, secrets, anything. There was so much that was lost about the city of Constantine. It had been destroyed by fire twice and by invasion six times. The palace itself was nothing more than ruins. Only the church had survived, and this only because it had been turned into a mosque.

They climbed another set of dank worn stairs and emerged into a time of wonder. Dawn cast a net of pearl light across the eastern sky. There was not a breath of wind. Venus still glimmered far to the west. The moon was a crescent, almost lost to the mist that rose off the Sea of Marmara.

Muriel thought she knew where they were. A small audience hall had fronted the waters between the church and the palace, assumed by archeologists to have been used by the vizier. It was rubble now, as were the broad stone steps leading to the water. Down below, where the stairs met the sea, the royal barge would have been moored. In its place now was a fisherman's craft with four oars lashed to the gunnels.

The acolyte pointed to the boat, bowed a silent farewell, and departed. They were left alone with the dawn.

The vizier shifted the sleeping child he carried from one arm to the other. "Should we not be setting out?"

Senator Bryan clicked open his pocket watch. "Another half hour."

"But we could—"

"We are safe here, and the timing is crucial." He slipped the watch back into his vest pocket. "Patience."

Wordlessly, Charles descended the stairs leading to the sea. Muriel hesitated, then handed the reliquary to Senator Bryan and followed him down. The waters lapped softly at her feet, and the rising mist was pale and soft as newfound hope. She asked, "Are you all right?"

Charles did not respond. His eyes carried the solemnity of the grave.

She decided not to press him. She turned and looked back at the vista rising from the dawn shadows. The fortress wall was crumbling such that it rose and fell like stone waves. Of the great tower that had once been the tallest lighthouse in the East, marking the official entrance to the Bosphorus Strait, there was nothing but a stubby root. She continued her slow turning, out to where the minarets rose like fragile fingers into the sunrise. Gradually the hills took on shape, rising into the new day.

Charles muttered, "All is lost. Everything adrift beyond the fog of..."

Muriel turned back to him and waited.

"It all seemed so clear to me once. All the lies and the fables."

"They are not lies," she said softly.

He looked at her. His gaze burned hot from within the dark cave of sleeplessness and worry. "You color your world with myths."

"They are not lies," she repeated. "Your wife knew this as well."

"Yes, and look where it got her. And me. And our child." He flung his arm at the rising fog. "Everything is gone. All of it. And I am left with..."

He wanted to tell her something. She could see that, and could also see that pressing him would do no good. So she spoke what was on her heart instead. "It isn't what is lost that troubles you, is it?"

He blinked at her, his face twisted in what might have been taken as raw fury.

"You set aside your faith when you buried your wife. You have spent these last weeks and months convincing yourself that it was all a lie. That the motives of believers are not true. That self-sacrifice and faith and love and compassion and hope are all myths."

"You know nothing about me," he snarled.

"I know you are in pain. I know you need healing. I know you hunger for it as much as you fear it." She reached out then. She could feel the eyes of the others on them, and she did not care. She touched his arm. She could almost feel the feverish fury burn through her fingertips. "Pray with me, Charles."

The fury left him, an abrupt draining away. She could sense the difference through her hand. He went from stone to broken humanity in the space of one long shuddering breath. "It is too late."

"Look at me. So long as there is life, there is hope. The offer of healing is constant. It is *eternal.*"

"You don't know what I have done."

"Charles, there is no distance so great that Jesus cannot cross. No divide made by man that cannot be filled by his loving grace."

"You do not know this."

"I do. With all my heart and mind, with the sinews of my body and the fiber of my being, I *know* this."

He stared at her a long moment, then glanced behind her and snarled anew. All the force and anger and power surged back. "Down!"

"What—"

He gripped her shoulder and flung her down. As she fell to the stone jetty, she looked back and saw a man perched upon the ruined parapet. One she instantly recognized. "That man followed me in Paris!"

"*Down, down, everybody down!*" Charles bounded up the stairs, pulling the pistol from his holster. As he moved, the man on the parapet unlimbered a rifle and slipped it into position.

In a flash, Muriel understood. How Charles had gone after the man while she had waited on the Paris bridge, and they had not seen him again. Not because Charles had frightened him off. Because Charles had told the man to hide himself better.

The man slipped a bullet into the chamber and took aim at her.

Charles fired. Again. A chip of stone burst from in front of the gun barrel. The man on the parapet cursed and called in French, "What are you doing?"

"Get away!"

The children wailed as Charles fired again. The attacker yelled in pain, then fired back.

Charles gasped once and fell like a stone.

"*No!*"

"Stay down!" Thomas Bryan pulled a short-barreled revolver from his pocket and fired up. The angle made his shot go wide, but it was enough to spoil the attacker's attempt to fire down at Muriel. The senator was joined by the vizier's son, Yussuf, who crawled away from his shrieking mother and fired with his own pistol.

Muriel crawled over to where Charles sprawled across two steps. A faint trace of red touched the corner of his mouth. He looked at her and tried to speak, but could not. Muriel took the gun from his slack fingers and aimed across his chest. She had shot her father's hunting rifle but never even held a pistol before. The recoil startled her. She steadied her aim and emptied the chamber. The attacker kept his head down until the firing pin clicked on an empty gun. But as he raised up once more, Thomas Bryan and Yussuf were both angled so as to see him. They fired together. The man was flung backward.

The air stunk of cordite and terror. Thomas Bryan raced back to where the vizier's family cowered. "We must flee!"

"Is he..."

"The shooter is down, but there could be others. Yussuf!"

"Coming!" The young man crouched over his pistol, filling the chamber with bullets from his pocket.

"Leave that for later!"

"Do as he says, my son."

Muriel shrilled, "Help me lift Charles!"

The senator and the vizier's son took hold of the limp Frenchman and together they maneuvered him into the boat. It was a broad-beamed wooden vessel that remained steady even with all of them aboard. Muriel unlashed the front hawser while Yussuf untied the stern. The three men set the oars in place as Muriel cradled Charles's head in her lap.

"On my count," the senator said. "Lower your blades, pull, lift, forward, lower, pull. Good!"

They drew slowly away from the dock. Gradually the fortress walls and the ruins faded from sight. Muriel thought she saw another head peek over the parapet, but the oars creaked and the men huffed and they drew safely into the fog.

The vizier's wife slipped to the bench beside Muriel and pulled back the jacket. Muriel stroked Charles's face and tried not to look at the spreading stain of red across his chest. "Can you do anything?"

Shayla looked at her but did not speak. The silence was horrible. Muriel did not realize she was crying until the tears dropped onto Charles's face.

He looked at her, his gaze as clear as it had been that morning in Notre Dame. He whispered, "Forgive me. I wish..." He stopped. And shuddered. And was gone.

: CHAPTER 26 :

:

The wooden vessel was perhaps thirty feet long and contained a mast and boom and lateen sail. They used the much-repaired canvas as a shroud and lay Charles in the empty bow. Muriel asked to take her hand at the oars. Yussuf took his father's place, and Thomas Bryan slipped behind the tiller. The oars creaked, and the wavelets splashed. And Muriel's silent tears continued to fall.

The mist tore into soft fragments and began to vanish. The clearer the morning grew, the more worried Thomas Bryan became. He called ahead, "Do you see anything?"

"There are boats everywhere," the vizier replied. "But none seem aimed in our direction."

"That's as good as we could hope for," Thomas Bryan replied. "Keep a sharp eye out, all of you."

"I don't understand," Shayla said. "Are we not waiting to be rescued?"

"Soon." Senator Bryan checked his pocket watch. "We are early."

The vizier asked, "Are we in position?"

"Directly off the Seraglio Point, lined up with the Golden Hind," the senator confirmed.

The vizier's wife demanded, "Then whom do you search the waters for?"

The vizier responded, "Charles acted on someone else's orders."

"But Charles did not attack us!"

"Shah, my wife, the children."

"Tell me what you mean."

"Charles reported our movements to his superiors. They arranged for the attacker to strike when we were most vulnerable. They will have accomplices in place in case we escaped."

Shayla was seated between Muriel and the stern. The two younger children were clustered about her, stretched out on the bench to either side so they could nestle in their mother's arms. "But why would they want to harm my children?"

"You know the answer to that as well as I, my beloved." He spoke with the soothing tone a parent would use on a fretful child.

Shayla cast a frightened glance at Muriel, then at the shrouded body in the nose of the boat. She clutched the children closer to her and did not speak.

The vizier went on, "We are pawns. The French want to use our capture to ingratiate themselves with the caliph. And if not with the caliph, then with Atatürk. Whoever holds power at the end of this struggle. The French cannot simply permit the others to gain control over the Turkish straits—"

Yussuf spoke softly, "I see something."

"Where?"

"Behind us. A shape in the mist. It's gone now. Perhaps I was…"

The remaining mist had separated and reformed into clumps. The thickest portions clung to the water like white islands, one of which was directly behind them. A shadow took form at its heart and grew until it split the mist apart. Out of the mist loomed a great steel shape. From its masthead fluttered the flag known as the Tricolor.

"The French have found us," the vizier moaned. "All is lost."

"Not yet," the senator exclaimed. "See there!"

But the direction he pointed was into the sun. The glare off the water was blinding. "I see nothing!"

"They are coming! Stand up and wave!"

But the vizier's arms were not enough. He stripped off his coat and waved it like a flag. "Are you certain?"

In response, the air was pierced by the fierce wail of a battle-ship's claxon. The roar of the American vessel's engines could be heard now, the deep thrum booming through Muriel's chest. The French frigate slowed, then turned away, as though pretending it never had intended to approach them at all. Quietly it slipped back into the fogbank and vanished.

They were saved.

: CHAPTER 27 :

:

Muriel and Senator Bryan would travel to Southampton on the USS *Whipple*, a newly commissioned destroyer that served in the eastern Mediterranean. But first, they were required to wait at the temporary naval station outside Izmir for eleven days, while a growing number of Americans were rounded up. The reliquary was placed under armed guard in the commandant's office. That same afternoon, the vizier and his family were transferred to a refugee camp on Cyprus, from which they would be settled in the United States.

Their second day on base, the duty officers and base chaplain held a funeral service for Charles Fouchet. They had delayed in order to inform the French legate of Charles's death and to inquire if an official representative wished to attend. They received no reply.

The wind was brisk off the sea that afternoon, strong enough to cause the flags overhead to crack like rifle shots. Muriel thought Charles would have found the military-style service very fitting. She wept a few tears, mostly over the man she wished he might have become. She prayed he finally found peace. She prayed he was able to rejoin his wife and child. She prayed for herself. The pain was far worse than she had expected. Senator

Bryan proved a dear friend throughout, remaining at her side while she silently bade the man farewell.

Muriel did not mind either the delays or the increasingly cramped conditions. The two barracks assigned to the refugees were little more than raw timber. Wind whistled through cracks in the walls. The nights were very cold.

Thankfully, it rained only once during that period. The seamen and soldiers assigned to assist them were cheerful and mostly polite, though several of them flirted outrageously. At least, they did until Senator Bryan visited on the fourth day, accompanied by the company commandant.

The news Thomas brought with him was grim. Atatürk continued to progress westward. The parliament in Ankara adopted a resolution to rename Constantinople. Once the conquest of western Turkey was completed, the city would become known as Istanbul, a title first used by early Ottoman rulers that meant "to find Islam."

Twice Muriel was invited to dine with Senator Bryan in the officers' mess. She could have gone every night, but in truth she preferred what the other women called barracks' duties. She helped prepare the meals, she tended fretting babies, she even served duty as a nurse's aide. But mostly she sat on the bench under the front awning and reflected on all that had happened.

She prayed for Charles. Her heart felt as heavy as lead. The one time she mentioned it to Senator Bryan, he grimly told her that soldiers returning from war often described such a feeling. Some veterans were now referring to it as survivor's guilt. But Muriel was not interested in hearing how it was described. She was *living* it. Even so, the senator's quiet sympathy did much to ease her burden.

It was not until they were on board the destroyer and plying their way through the sunlit Aegean that Muriel felt able to thank the senator. Thomas Bryan seemed genuinely surprised by her words. "What on earth for?"

"Everything," she replied. "I will find a better way to say this in the days to come. But right now, I want you to know that your trust in me has transformed my life."

He inspected her with gentle concern. "Despite your recent woes, you still feel this?"

"I do. So much." She knew there was a great deal more that needed saying. But not then, not while so many others milled about the steel deck. For now, she made do with simply, "You were right about Charles."

Senator Bryan must have seen her struggle to maintain control, for he leaned in close enough to fill her vision and said quietly, "And I was right about you, my dear."

• • •

Once they arrived in Southampton, they spent two nights in a seafront hotel that had most definitely seen better days. It had served as a way station for officers going to the western front. Current renovations were hampered by a scarcity of skilled workers and materials. The dining hall smelled of fresh paint while the rooms were damp and slightly mildewed. But after the barracks, followed by four days on board an overcrowded destroyer, Muriel was thrilled to simply have a bit of privacy.

On the third day in England, everything changed.

The SS *Bismarck* had been completed in 1914, though its final fitting was delayed by the start of the Great War. In 1920, it was ceded to Great Britain by the Treaty of Versailles. The vessel was

renamed the RMS *Majestic* and went into service for the White
Star company. As they waited to board, Senator Bryan informed
her that the reliquary was already stowed in the ship captain's
private safe. He then explained that the *Majestic* was the largest
and most elegant of a new range of oceangoing vessels known
as *liners*. Muriel had no idea what that actually meant until a
white-gloved purser ushered them on board.

The entrance foyer was thirty feet high and illuminated by
a crystal chandelier that, according to the purser, weighed
almost two tons. The swimming pool was eighty feet long with
a stained-glass ceiling and Roman columns lining all four sides.
The purser informed Muriel that she and the other upper-deck
ladies had the magnificent chamber all to themselves for two
hours each afternoon. The first-class dining salon was a perfect
oval almost two hundred feet long. She and the senator had
adjoining rooms and would share a butler. The only word to
describe her cabin was *exquisite*.

Senator Bryan had received an urgent telegram just before
they boarded, requesting he make a formal report to the White
House as soon as they returned. He spent the first three days
of their transatlantic voyage locked in his cabin. He even took
his meals there. Twice he emerged and tried to apologize, but
Muriel assured him that she truly relished this solitude. The
ship's library was magnificent, almost as large as the first-class
dining hall. The waiters grew accustomed to Muriel's dining
with three or four books for company.

At night when the ship slept, she wrote three letters. One was
to the French prime minister, the second to the interior minister,
and the third to Charles himself. The pages were so smeared
with her tears she doubted anyone would be able to read her

script. Which scarcely mattered, since she was uncertain any of them would ever be mailed.

The ship endured a late spring squall, with lashing rain and gale-force winds. Muriel gratefully accepted their steward's offer of a slicker and walked miles around the empty decks. Huge waves battered the vessel, or tried to, but the *Majestic* plowed through them with stately grace. Muriel especially loved the gray-streaked dawns, when a pale wash of light defied the clouds and the storm. The promise of hope in the midst of life's tempest was unmistakable. Inwardly, she argued with Charles, she missed him, and gradually she found a way to say farewell.

Toward dawn on their fourth day at sea, Muriel dreamed once more of standing before the cross. The image came and went as swiftly as the indrawn breath that drew her awake. She lay there for a time, then rose and dressed and took the mystery out to the storm-swept deck. As the light strengthened into a tumultuous dawn, she grew increasingly certain that she understood what was meant by her dream.

That evening, their last at sea, she and Senator Bryan were guests of the captain. She dressed formally for dinner, and he emerged from his cabin in the new evening wear called a dinner jacket. He bowed over her hand, complimented her anew on the Chanel gown, and escorted her with the proud bearing of a favorite uncle. But Muriel found the dinner conversation rather boring. A trio of pompous ladies discussed the goings-on of people Muriel neither knew nor cared about. After dessert was served, an orchestra began playing at the room's opposite end. Senator Bryan rose from his position by the captain and asked, "My dear, would you care to dance?"

The senator might be adept at many things, but he was no dancer. Muriel allowed herself to be rocked slightly back and forth, with no connection whatsoever to the music's rhythm. When the song ended, he asked, "Shall we resume our places at the table?"

"If we must."

He smiled at her lack of enthusiasm. "I feared your companions would prove rather rough going."

"Worse than the gale," Muriel agreed.

"Then let's move to the bar. I want to have a word."

The bar was an adjoining chamber that ran along the ship's starboard side. Great windows flashed regularly with lightning, revealing whitecaps and rain-spattered glass. Senator Bryan asked a servant for a private table and ordered coffee for them both. "Forgive me for coming straight to the point. But I expect officials from the White House to be on hand when we dock in New York tomorrow. I will be sequestered with them for the duration of our train journey to Washington. And there is still work for me to complete this evening."

"I understand."

He nodded his thanks to the waiter who deposited their coffees, waited for him to depart, then said, "You have shown yourself to be a most remarkable ally, Muriel. And under the most difficult of circumstances."

She replied honestly, "I would not have missed this for the world."

"Despite all the traumas, the dangers, the..." He searched for the proper word. "Disappointments?"

In the dining salon next door, the orchestra began to play Schubert. The last time Muriel had heard that particular melody had been in the Élysée Palace. She smiled against the burn to her eyes. "What disappointment would that be?"

Thomas Bryan leaned back in his seat, clearly pleased by her response. "Might I ask what you intend to do upon your return?"

"I assume my position at the Smithsonian is still open," she replied.

"You may rest assured I will see to that." He toyed with his cup. "If that is indeed what you desire."

Muriel felt the slightest tremor race through her frame, as though one of the giant ocean waves had managed to reach into this refined salon and shake her world.

Senator Bryan continued, "It has been three years since the women of America won the right to vote. A move that was far too long in coming."

"You were at the vanguard of that process," Muriel recalled. "My father and I heard you address the Senate before the amendment was ratified. I was moved to tears."

"There are momentous events taking shape in Washington," the senator continued. "Matters that will shape the world for generations to come. I would like you to come be a part of this."

Muriel felt frozen to her seat.

"There will be resistance," he warned. "The idea of women holding positions of importance within our government will face strong headwinds. But I have had the chance to test your mettle during our journey, and I am convinced that you are up to the task."

She found it difficult to swallow, much less respond.

"I'm not certain what precise role you would best be suited for," he went on. "It will most likely come down to where I and my allies decide your presence will have the most impact. The White House is one option. Or as an aide to one of the key Senate committees. Most likely I will appoint you to my personal staff and then see what door opens in the days to come."

Muriel turned to the rain-spattered window and watched as lightning illuminated the distant clouds.

"Might I ask what you think of my proposal?"

She replied slowly, "My father told me that he hoped the world would hear of me because of both my abilities and my faith."

"Your father is a forward-thinking man," Senator Bryan replied and rapped his fingers upon the table. "Then is it settled?"

. . .

ABOUT THE AUTHOR

Davis Bunn, a professional novelist for twenty-four years, has sales in excess of seven million copies in twenty languages. His titles have appeared on numerous national bestseller lists, and his titles have been Main or Featured Selections with every major U.S. bookclub. Davis serves as Writer-In-Residence at Regent's Park College, Oxford University, and has served as Lecturer in Oxford's creative writing program. In 2011, his novel *Lion of Babylon* was named a Best Book of the Year by *Library Journal*. The sequel, *Rare Earth,* won Davis his fourth Christy Award for Excellence in Fiction in 2013. In 2014, Davis was granted the Lifetime Achievement award by the Christy board of judges.